Wild Child

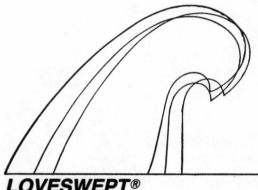

LOVESWEPT®

Suzanne Forster
Wild Child

Doubleday

NEW YORK • LONDON • TORONTO • SYDNEY • AUCKLAND

LOVESWEPT®

Published simultaneously in hardcover by Doubleday
and in paperback by Bantam which are divisions of
Bantam Doubleday Dell Publishing Group, Inc.,
666 Fifth Avenue, New York, New York 10103

Loveswept, Doubleday and the portrayal of the wave device
are registered trademarks of
Bantam Doubleday Dell Publishing Group, Inc.

If you would be interested in receiving a walnut finish
book rack for your Loveswept books, please write
to this address for information:

Loveswept
Bantam Books
P.O. Box 985
Hicksville, NY 11802

Library of Congress Cataloging-in-Publication Data
Forster, Suzanne.
    Wild child / by Suzanne Forster. — 1st hardbound ed.
        p.   cm.
    ISBN 0-385-41270-3
    I. Title.
PS3556.07443W5   1990
813'.54—dc20   89-27329
                                                          CIP

This one's for Tara, whose support, enthusiasm, and generosity of heart have meant so much to me over the years.

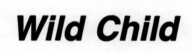

Wild Child

Prologue

His touch was rapture. She arched her neck, and the soft sound in her throat was plaintive. Longing, such longing. She'd dreamt of this for years, his touch, his kiss. Midnight surrounded them, deep purple drenched with the scent of lilacs. Stars shimmered above him, paling against the moondrift of silver eyes.

His fingers stroked her skin with fire. His breath murmured in her hair, teasing the mahogany tendrils. He rained a shower of kisses over her face, warming her temples, her closed eyelids, and at last, her mouth. She gasped softly at the taste of him. The nerve-spun sensation unfurling inside her was a need as sharp as life itself. Lord, don't let me want this so much, she thought, as his lips moved over hers. Don't let me need it.

A moan, deep and thrilling, coarsened his breathing.

His hands pushed through her hair, and she knew it was time. Another second in his arms and she wouldn't be able to go through with it. He breathed her name and the sound of it was torment. Agony. How long had she waited to hear him say her name that way? How long had she waited for this moment? Now! she thought, her heart surging. Somehow she had to do it now. Stop him, push him away, hurt him the way he'd hurt her! It was his turn to feel the knife edge of need. His time to bleed.

She twisted out of his arms with a muffled cry, and at the same time she found herself thrashing awake in her own bed.

Her body was filmed with perspiration as she sat up and flung off the bedcovers. A dream! She had had the dream . . . again.

"No subsequent humiliations can ever cut so deep as those of youth."
—Margaret Atwood, author of *The Cat's Eye*

One

CITY OF STRONG HEARTS the welcome sign claimed.

Catherine D'Angelo breathed in, then let the warmed air drain from her lungs. Excitement and apprehension mixed inside her. It was a mistake coming back, she knew that. But it was too late for second thoughts now. She was almost home!

As she swung her red Mustang convertible onto the main drag of Cameron Bay, Oregon, she was hit with a gust of memories so poignant she could hardly catch her breath. The town's landmarks flew by her: city hall, the old courthouse building. She slowed at a crosswalk, waiting for some laughing teenagers to pass, and her eyes were drawn to another ghost ship from her past. Bayside High School's brick facade was piercingly familiar, from the cracks separating the letters to the pine trees dripping brown needles onto the street.

Everything was just as she remembered it, and the sense of sameness brought the changes within her into sharp contrast. It had been ten years since she'd set foot in Cameron Bay. She was a different woman now. *But would anyone who remembered her believe that?*

Moments later she pulled into the parking lot of the West End Youth Center, with an uneasy sense of destiny. In her fantasies she was the conquering heroine come home, but now, staring at the converted, ranch-style building, she felt more like the criminal returned to the scene of the crime. The center was an outreach agency for disaffected teenagers, and its small staff of licensed psychologists were trained to handle a wide variety of problems: runaways, broken homes, even juvenile criminal offenses.

In her own "disaffected" teenage years, Cat had fit into the last category.

If someone had asked her at that moment why she'd returned, she couldn't have answered them, although she had a logical explanation. She needed supervised counseling hours to qualify for her psychotherapist's license, and her own former counselor, Gwen Winters, had convinced her to spend the late spring and summer working at the center. "Who better to help troubled kids than the original," Gwen had argued. That was the explanation. But was it the reason?

As she cut the car's engine, she reminded herself that she was there to help, not to be helped. She had a master's degree now. She was a professional.

She glanced in the rearview mirror and smoothed a few wayward strands of mahogany hair into the French knot coiled at her nape. A feathering of copper blush defined her cheekbones, and a light application of mascara separated her naturally thick, dark lashes. Tweaking the crisp white collar of her blouse, she scrutinized the way it set off the apricot tones of her complexion. She looked well groomed, thrifty, and punctual, a model of propriety. Yes, she *had* changed.

"Catherine!" The name fairly bounced along the air waves.

Catherine slipped out of the car and saw Gwen Winters hurrying toward her, arms outstretched. The sight brought such a welling of emotion that for a moment Catherine couldn't navigate. This was the homecoming she'd imagined so many times. *Now don't get sappy,* she told herself, but her eyes misted with tears anyway. She took a jerky step and opened her arms to her former counselor, laughing as they embraced. "Oh, Gwen, I've missed you." She hugged the plumpish woman with all of her strength.

"Come in, darling, come in," Gwen cried breathlessly, urging Catherine toward the building. "I've got some fresh lemonade with orange slices, just the way you like it."

Once inside, the two women reacquainted themselves over tall glasses of iced lemonade and lingering reminiscences. Catherine went first at Gwen's insistence, bringing her friend and mentor up to date since their last exchange of letters.

"Yes, I did buy myself some new clothes," she told Gwen, anticipating her friend's question as she finished her recap. "And no, I'm still not dating. I don't have time!"

"Catherine, you're going to shrivel up!"

"Speaking of which," Catherine came back, "how's the diet going?"

Now it was Gwen's turn to "fess up," and by the time she was through, the two women were laughing and exchanging gossipy tidbits like sorority sisters. But when their conversation wound down, Catherine sobered. "I hope you're right about this pilgrimage," she said. "I'm not at all sure Cameron Bay is ready for the return of its prodigal daughter. Or that *I'm* ready."

"We all have to face our demons sooner or later, darling." Gwen brushed some imaginary dust from the coffee table they were sitting at and shifted in her chair. "And speaking of demons, did I tell you that he'll be dropping by soon, to pick up a file on one of our clients?"

"He? Who?"

"Blake Wheeler."

If Catherine hadn't been sitting, Gwen would have had to scrape her up off the floor. "Blake Wheeler is coming here? *Why?*" She stared at Gwen incredulously, then spun up and away from the table. "Why, Gwen, *why?*"

Gwen's lemonade hit the glass-topped table with a surprised clink. "Goodness, I'd almost forgotten how dramatic you are, dear. Blake's the district attorney, though I doubt you've forgotten. One of our clients is to be a witness for the prosecution." She smiled. "Nice to be on the right side of the law for a change, isn't it?"

Catherine wasn't mollified. "I won't be here."

"Oh, Cat, you can't avoid him forever. It's a small town."

"My name isn't Cat! It's Catherine—" Seeing the stricken expression on Gwen's face, she cut off the tirade. "I'm sorry, Gwen, but I hate that man! You *know* how I hate that man."

"Catherine, really—all this anger, I think—"

"He's slick and cold," Cat said with conviction. "He's ruthless, Gwen. How do you expect me to feel about the man? My father lost his life in the Wheeler Lumber Mill! Through their negligence, sheer negligence."

Gwen's voice took on a note of reproach. "You can't blame Blake for something his father did. Lord, the boy was only twenty-two at the time, Cat. He broke with his family over that accident, and you know it."

Cat knew what was coming next. The Blake Wheeler legend: how he'd made personal restitution to the survivors, how he was still paying their medical expenses. "A regular hero, right," she muttered, "always the conquering hero."

Cat jammed her hands into her slacks' pockets and glowered out the window at the sun peeking through the drizzly horizon. If she had to hear one more time how Blake Wheeler was the lifeblood of this town, how he was marked for greatness, she was going to scream! As far as she was concerned, the local newspapers Gwen had sent her were propaganda, pure propaganda. "Why does everyone here seem to think Blake Wheeler is the best thing since Charlton Heston played Moses, Gwen? Believe me, the man isn't perfect. He's a flawed human being, just like the rest of us."

Gwen sighed. "Own up, Cat," she said at last. "We both know why you really hate him."

The room froze with silence. Astounded, Catherine gripped the back of the chair she'd been sitting in and stopped herself just short of the collision force she felt inside. Tears stung at her eyelids. "Not fair, Gwen, not fa—" The last word snapped off as the center door opened and slammed shut behind her.

Catherine pivoted, her pulse running riot inside a flash-frozen body. As Gwen bustled over to greet their visitor, Catherine stared at the tall, golden-haired man balefully. Of course it was him, Blake Wheeler, the chosen one, the man to lead Cameron Bay and perhaps even the state of Oregon into the 1990s.

A moment later, as Gwen wrapped up her chat with Wheeler and seemed inclined to bring him over, Catherine's jaw locked along with her body. She couldn't help it. Put simply, she loathed and detested the man. Years ago he had brought her the greatest heartbreak and humiliation of her young life. Because of deputy district attorney Blake Wheeler, she had served two years in Purdy Hall, the state reformatory.

Catherine was hot-blooded by nature, but she wasn't vindictive. That trait didn't run in her family, and it wasn't in her makeup either. And yet if she had ever nurtured vengeance in her heart for anyone, she nurtured it for him.

"Catherine, you remember Blake Wheeler, don't you?" Gwen's voice was hopeful.

As Wheeler and Gwen walked toward her, Catherine was given a gift. Speech. "How could I forget," she said, icing down each word like an athlete ices her injuries. Amazed at her own resilience, she released the chair she was still gripping with one hand. "Yes, I remember." Every wretched detail, she thought, staring into his steel-gray eyes. The aggressively handsome features, the Kennedy-like charisma, the ruthless heart. She remembered it all. And to think that once, long ago, she had adored this man. *Adored him.*

"You've changed," he said, assessing her quietly. "Radically." The gloom of the day hid whatever might have been concealed in the depths of his eyes.

"Yes, hasn't she," Gwen put in. "She's right on the brink of qualifying for her counseling license. A brilliant student, Catherine is, Berkeley, Phi Beta Kappa."

"I never doubted it."

His voice was smooth, rangy, warm with amusement. *Never doubted it?* Catherine nearly gasped with outrage. This sacrilege from the man who'd put her in the slammer?! "Oh, now I get it." She slapped her forehead, a gesture sharply reminiscent of her Italian father. "I see how it goes! When you suspect a child is destined for greatness, you let her cool her heels in the state reformatory for a couple of years. Character building, right?"

He was obviously unprepared for her broadside. "Cat—"

"My name isn't Cat!"

Gwen fluttered around them. "Blake, you look parched, dear. Wouldn't you like some lemonade? How about you, Catherine? A refill?"

Locked in visual combat, neither Catherine or Blake responded. From somewhere outside the center, a car horn blared, accentuating the barbed silence. The sound brought Cat up short. Forcibly reclaiming her errant emotions, she willed the ice floe back into her veins. She could not let herself fall apart with this man. *She could not.*

"Well, fine then," Gwen said uncertainly. "I'll just run to the kitchen and get the pitcher."

As Gwen disappeared, Blake stepped away from the window.

Catherine jerked back, rigidly maintaining the distance between them. At least she could see him clearly now. She registered his physical changes with a pounding heart and some surprise. He'd been twenty-six when she left, so he had to be thirty-six now. Time had improved him physically, she had to admit. If someone liked tall, muscular men with tons of burnished gold hair and a ruddy, sunswept look, that is. She didn't. Not anymore. She also didn't like his opened-neck shirt, the fashionably loosened tie, or the way his shirtsleeves were rolled up above his elbows. On another man it might have looked virile, even sexy. On Blake Wheeler it looked too damn much like a "have" trying to be a "have not."

How did he get that incredible tan? she wondered resentfully. He had the physique of a man who battled alligators in his spare time, and yet, she sincerely doubted that he ever set a foot outside except to play tennis at the country club. Image, she reasoned, anything for the ol' political image when you were shooting to be governor of the state someday. He probably even had a tanning machine in his bedroom.

While Catherine was ticking off Blake's physical shortcomings and character flaws, he was taking in her transformation in a rather different way. The surprise she felt was magnified in him by a factor of ten. He could hardly believe the rebellious sixteen-year-old he'd tried and found guilty for car theft had become a woman. Lord help them all, a formidable woman. Her eyes were dark and glittery with anger. The lush hair he remembered was restrained almost painfully in a knot at the nape of her neck. She was tall, slim as a whip, and rigid as a pitchfork. But what fascinated him was her facade of icy indifference.

Her body posture, her attitude said, "Live or die,

fella, I could not care less." She was glacial. She was aloof. But her eyes. Under the ice, her eyes were flamethrowers. He'd never seen such cold fury in a woman before. Or a man, for that matter. If she'd been anyone else, he would have talked it all out, but in her case his instincts told him to go slow. The woman was a walking bundle of contradictions. She was a powder keg.

"What I meant earlier," he said, choosing his words carefully, "was that I knew you were going to be extraordinary in some way, but I didn't expect this."

"This?" she said suspiciously. "What's *this*?"

The word that flashed to mind was "ferocity." He knew telling her would be like setting a match to the powder. Besides, it was more than anger that made her compelling. Much more.

He considered the proud set of her shoulders and the boyish cut of her cotton twill slacks and couldn't find the words. "When I get it figured out, I'll let you know. Whatever it is, it looks good on you."

Cat faltered for just a second. Why had he said that? There must be a reason. The man she remembered didn't do anything without a reason. "I'm sure you didn't come by to bask in my self-assurance."

"Actually, I came by to pick up a file on one of Gwen's clients, Johnny Drescher."

"I'll get it for you." She had no idea where it was, but any excuse to leave would do at the moment. Any excuse.

"Cat—Catherine."

Startled, she swung around to face him. Her first impression was of gray eyes shot with silver, and male features so sharply etched in her memory that just to look at him brought her a glancing pain.

"Maybe we ought to talk—you know, clear some things up."

She held his gaze, and all the biting things she'd ever wanted to say to him ran through her mind. The air in her chest felt squeezed into a tight little tangle beneath her breastbone. "I'd rather not."

As she turned away to look for the file, she could feel herself shaking. Frustration lumped in her throat. After all the years of dreaming about a head-on confrontation with Cameron Bay's DA, she'd wimped out! She hadn't said any of the things she'd been burning to say. Not the *important* things anyway. And she wasn't even sure why. All she'd known was that she couldn't bare the thought of exposing herself to him, not the fury in her heart, or the truth of how badly he'd hurt her.

Fortunately, she saw the file he wanted lying on top of a two-drawer cabinet. As she went to pick it up, Gwen returned with the pitcher of lemonade and a plate of cookies.

"Peanut butter, anyone? A snickerdoodle?" Gwen's breezy calm belied a less-than-steady grip as she refilled the glasses sitting on the coffee table.

"No thanks," Blake said, "I've got to be going."

Catherine had returned with the file and offered it to him, but Blake didn't take it. Instead, he let his gaze drift from the dainty button cuff of her sleeve to the crisp white collar of her blouse. Pretty prim stuff for such an exotic creature, he thought.

"Pretrial hearing's at one," he added, watching her flush as he ignored her outstretched hand. Years of courtroom theatrics had taught him timing. He'd learned the power of strategic silence, of making people wait for your next word, or move. By now it was a reflex.

Catherine glanced at her watch and thrust the file at him. "You're late."

Eyeing them both, Gwen tweaked the folder from Catherine's hand, gently swung Blake around, and escorted him to the door. "Give a holler when you're ready to meet with Johnny," she told him, slipping the file under his arm. "I'll set something up."

Blake nodded. "My office might be best," he said, and then he departed without a backward glance.

Gwen shut the door behind him and peered over her shoulder at Catherine. "Well?"

"Well what?"

"How did it go, silly? I heard you two talking. He's changed, don't you think?"

"Changed?" Catherine pulled at her blouse collar, freeing it from the odd dampness around her neck. "Yes, I suppose a moment of reflection *is* quite a change for a man without a conscience."

Gwen rolled her eyes. Hopeless, her expression said.

But Catherine never saw her friend's gesture. She was staring past Gwen, out the center's window. She was watching her sworn enemy get into his midnight-blue Corvette and drive away. She remembered his interest, and especially his perplexity when he was trying to describe how she'd changed.

The truth was it astounded her to think she could make a man like Blake Wheeler question himself, even for a moment.

Blake downshifted the Corvette Stingray into low gear and slowly released the clutch, letting the fuel-injected engine roar and vibrate like an oncoming train. The gearshift trembled in his hand. The car was straining to be given its head, and Blake savored the moment, the chained momentum. Residual energy coursed up his arm, reverberated in his thighs. It was the dynamic tension between power controlled and power unleashed that intrigued him. In machinery, in people, in all of life. A dangerous preoccupation for a man with political ambitions, he knew, but then, he'd always preferred the danger zone.

He'd curbed that instinct very successfully in the last several years. He'd gone along with the king-makers who saw him as political gold and made all the right career moves. But through it all, he'd never quite extinguished the notion that some men were destined to dance near the fires of discovery, to see how close they could come without getting burned.

As he drove through the quiet, shaded streets of Cameron Bay, heading toward the courthouse, Blake thought about the fire he'd just rediscovered, Cat D'Angelo. On impulse, he pulled off the main drag and took a series of side roads until he hit a deserted stretch leading out of town. Double-shifting into fifth, he wound the Stingray's engine up to 6,000 rpms and let her fly. The speed spiked his heartbeat like an adrenaline burst.

When he finally brought the car to a shuddering stop, it occurred to him that if a woman could be like a car, then she was like the machine beneath him: sleek, fast, demanding. Or maybe that was his fantasy.

In truth, he didn't know who Catherine D'Angelo was. He was trained to read body language, to probe beneath the surface for truth. Once, a long time ago, he'd thought he had her pegged. But now, in all her adult female glory, she was sending out so many signals he couldn't get a fix on her.

There had been traces of vulnerability. Once, when she'd averted her eyes, he thought he'd seen a quiver of something sad in her mouth. It had made his stomach clutch, that glimpse of fragility, of softness. It had made him realize that her ferocity was protecting something tender and breakable inside her. Or maybe that was his fantasy too.

He felt the tightness in his chest again and realized he was feeling more than concern. It was guilt. For a second she'd looked like an injured child who couldn't or wouldn't, admit to the pain. How much of that pain was he responsible for? How much of her anger and sadness could be laid right at the feet of Blake Wheeler?

A memory of the trial and its firebrand of a defendant flickered before him. Sixteen-year-old Cat D'Angelo had been hostile and uncooperative from the first, refusing to give testimony against her partner in crime, an unsavory eighteen-year-old named Cheryl. He'd had a hunch Cat wasn't involved in the theft but no proof. He'd promised her immunity in exchange for her testimony, but she'd refused. The truth was, she'd infuriated him with her recalcitrance. Settling back into the bucket seat, he reflected on the rest of it, and how she'd shocked the hell out of him with some of her other tactics.

He drifted for several moments, remembering, before a car passed and reminded him that he was idling alongside the highway—and that he'd forgotten all about the pretrial hearing!

He hit the gas, made a U-turn, and headed toward town. There were a lot of things about her case that had disturbed him, but it was what he'd learned afterward that haunted him the most. Her father had been one of the five men killed in the Wheeler lumber mill accident three years earlier.

That information had hit him like a blow. It had even forced him to reexamine his tactics. He'd been the new hire with the DA's office—a virgin—and Cat D'Angelo's trial was his first time up. They were all waiting to see if Harlon Wheeler's kid could cut the mustard in court. Blake had needed a conviction.

Shifting the car into cruise, he flexed his shoulders to ease the tightening muscles in his neck. The memories were unpleasant at best. He'd been an ambitious SOB in those days, certainly not given to self-examination. But for weeks afterward, he was to wonder if he'd done the right thing. Finally he'd rationalized it in his mind. The evidence was there, hard and irrefutable. She'd been joyriding on I-5 in a stolen T-bird with Cheryl. The county sheriff had pulled them over. Both girls had been tried and convicted by a jury, and under the circumstances anything else would have been a travesty of justice.

He'd speculated often on how Cat D'Angelo might turn out. He remembered thinking even as he'd questioned her in the witness stand that she was extraordinary in many ways. Some women were beautiful, others were alluring. At sixteen, Cat was already the kind of woman who could drive a man to leave his family, or a ship captain to steer his vessel onto the rocks. There was a bewitching, temptresslike quality about her. A romantic poet would have called her a budding siren.

He often wondered if those very qualities had precipitated her downfall. During the trial it had come out that she had problems at home, with her mother. Precociousness and all that natural sensuality on a sixteen-year-old could be threatening to adults. It sure as hell had threatened him.

His thoughts veered to the unpredictable woman he'd just encountered in the West End Youth Center and he smiled grimly. Nothing had changed. Cat D'Angelo *was* the danger zone.

Two

"Ackerman's cheese puffs?! Gwen, thank you!"

Catherine gaped at the yellow and gold cellophane bags spilling out of the desk drawer she'd just opened. Somehow Gwen must have known that an emergency supply of her favorite junk food was just what she needed to decompress from the shock of her homecoming.

"Enjoy!" Gwen's voice sailed back from somewhere in the building.

Catherine tore open a sack, popped a buttery cheese curl into her mouth, and sighed with relief. Ackerman's were a local delicacy and highly prized by Cameron Bay's younger set. Cat had picked up the habit in her grade-school days and had never been able to kick it. Fortunately, Gwen had shipped them to her at Berkeley on a semiregular basis.

Munching intently, she sank into a chair that groaned even with the slight weight of her five-foot-six frame, kicked her feet up onto a badly scratched metal desk, and reconsidered the dingy room that was to be her office. Under the influence of Ackerman's, she allowed that the place wasn't as hopeless as she'd originally thought. A brass nameplate on her desk and diplomas hanging on the wall would shine things up nicely. She sampled another cheese curl and nodded her head reflectively. Not half bad, her office, small though it was, bare though it was.

By the time she'd finished off the snack, crumpling and tossing the bag into a wastebasket, she felt almost right with the world again. The cheese puffs even seemed to have taken the edge off her encounter with Blake Wheeler that morning, if such a thing was possible.

"Feel like talking?"

Cat raised her head to Gwen's smiling face in the doorway. "Sure, long as it's not about you know who."

"It's not. It's about you know what."

"What?"

"Your anger."

"My anger?"

"Yes, your anger toward you know who."

Cat groaned as her friend entered and pulled up a chair. "That's sneaky," she said, plucking up another bag of Ackerman's. She tore off the seal and held the bag out to Gwen.

Gwen shook her head. "Can't be bribed," she said, fixing Cat with a look that managed to convey both moral superiority and motherly concern. "You've got to do something about all that bottled-up anger, child."

Cat registered the twitch in her own cheek muscles, and deeper, the flame that flickered eternal in her heart. No use denying it, she decided as she bit the top off a cheese puff and chewed determinedly. "I am doing something about it, Gwen, I'm savoring it. Anger is the great motivator, you know that. It gives people courage, makes them do things they didn't think they were capable of." Like telling off arrogant district attorneys, she thought, which she definitely intended to do one day soon.

Gwen shook her head. She seemed to have missed completely the significance of Cat's argument.

"For some people, yes," she said, "but you've got too much energy bound up in resentment. You're a walking time bomb, Cat. You've got this crazy obsession about Blake Wheeler. Why, you act like you're the only person he ever sent to Purdy Hall." She shook her head. "Let go of your grudge, child, and get on with your life . . ."

Cat listened in silence as Gwen continued, the soul of reason. She knew her friend was right, of course. She'd been telling herself the very same thing for years. But Gwen didn't understand that things weren't that simple now that Cat had returned to Cameron Bay. Seeing Blake Wheeler in the flesh had brought back all the wounds, all the humiliations. It was worse than reliving the experiences; it was like having the past walk up and slap you in the face.

". . . the wisest thing you could do," Gwen was saying, "is to forgive and forget."

"Really?" Cat's voice was sharper than she intended. "Well, I've got an even moldier cliché for you: 'Easier said than done.' "

Gwen looked up in surprise, and suddenly Cat's heart was beating harder than she wanted it to. She'd done it again, struck out reflexively, and at the wrong person. Gwen cared about her. And Gwen might be the *only* person who did. Cat's throat tightened, and an apology formed on her lips. Finally, she just smiled . . . confused, bemused, sad.

Gwen's slow nod said she understood more than Cat realized, and the warmth in her eyes said yes, everything was okay. But Cat wasn't that easily consoled. She was thinking about all the careless ways people hurt each other without really meaning to, and how it was almost as painful to strike out as it was to be struck. Was it her personal curse to be born with a hot temper and a soft heart?

"Got the Cameron Bay blues, do you?" Gwen's voice was soft and calming as she rose and walked to Cat's chair. "I'm going to leave you alone now. I think that's probably best, and I've got some errands to run anyway." She placed a hand on Cat's shoulder. "Give yourself some time, Catherine."

Cat nodded, unable to look up at her friend. "Yeah, thanks," she said. There was a sting in her throat and some unsteadiness in her fingers as slowly, meticulously, one fold at a time, she sealed off the remaining cheese puffs and slipped the bag into the pocket of her slacks. Blues? It was *hell* coming back. There wasn't any other word for it but that one, hell.

Gwen's hand tightened on her shoulder and Cat swallowed thickly. No one else knew, or could know, how bad it was, not even Gwen. As tolerant and compassionate as her former counselor was, there were things she didn't understand—things Cat had never told her—the conflicts locked up inside, the confusion, the shame and helpless, self-directed fury. *Oh, Gwen, my good, kind friend,* Cat thought, *Purdy Hall isn't the only thing I can't forgive Blake Wheeler for.*

Gwen's hand lifted. "You okay?"

Cat nodded quickly. "Yup . . . go on now, get out of here. Do your errands."

As Gwen left, Cat swung her feet off the desk and wandered into the center's reception area. She could still feel Blake Wheeler's presence in the room. She could almost see him as though he were there, an energy field, a hologram. He certainly hasn't lost it, she thought. The press had described him more than once as a man of few words: "Silent and spellbinding," one article had said, "but compellingly articulate when he chooses to be." Another had reported his "killer charisma."

Whatever the quality was, Cat thought, he never had to resort to force to get what he wanted. He simply assumed sovereignty of whatever he touched, effortlessly. If he'd been Napoleon, the Prussians would have *given* him Waterloo!

The awareness set off a chain reaction of images in Cat's head, and a soft whorl of anxiety took shape inside her. There was only one time she'd seen Blake Wheeler lose his cool, and she didn't want to think about that now. No, she entreated silently, *not now.*

But she couldn't control the lightness or the inner agitation. Within seconds she felt the back of her neck grow hot as a decade-old memory insinuated its way into her thoughts . . .

His hand closed on her wrist and his gray eyes pierced her like a blade. He was angry with her. She could feel it in the heat of his skin, the grainy sound of his voice. But she sensed something else . . . a quickening, a current of energy. She reached out to touch him, and his fingers threatened to bruise her. "Don't," he warned her as a flash of desire electrified his silver eyes . . .

Cat forced the flashback from her mind, but her heart was beating as wildly as though it had just happened. She felt a twist of excitement in the pit of her stomach, and then almost as suddenly, the cold slap of shame.

A large bay window dominated the reception area. Cat walked to it, her hands unsteady as she pressed them to her mouth and stared out at the overcast sky. The raw intensity of the flashback had frightened her. But what disturbed her more was that suddenly she knew why she'd come back to Cameron Bay. The *real* reason. She'd returned to even the score with Blake Wheeler, because he deserved it, and to set him straight about Cat D'Angelo at all costs—because *she* deserved that.

"Revenge," she said, shivering at the chill that came off the glass, "such a messy business."

Still lost in her thoughts a few moments later, Cat didn't notice the forlorn figure making his way down the road that fronted the center. The thin, hunched boy was drab as a Dickens character, except for an unruly mop of dark hair with a red bandanna tied around it like a headband. It was only when a car roared up behind the boy and blasted its horn that Cat was jolted out of her reflections.

She watched with curiosity and some alarm as the shiny black Camaro, full of rowdy teenagers, slowed and kept pace with the shuffling boy. The car had a raccoon's tail dangling from its antenna, and Cat could just make out a Bayside High School letterman's sweater on a red-haired young man hanging out of the driver's-side window.

The car's horn honked repeatedly, and the kids jeered and hooted at the boy, calling out insults. "Hey, jailbird! Get out of town, you loser!" The boy didn't respond. Instead, he tucked in and walked faster, moving ahead of the car, and just as abruptly, the Camaro jerked forward and veered into his path, its horn blaring. The boy leapt away, and the car surged again, forcing him into a runoff ditch.

Heat rose in Cat's throat. Her first impulse was to storm outside and raise Cain with the young hoodlums, but she held herself back. The incidents with belligerent teenagers during her own trial had been torturous, but to have had an adult rush in and rescue her would only have made everything worse.

She watched the boy climb out of the shallow trench and face his attackers, and her chest tightened with anger and concern. She couldn't hear what was said, but she could see the angry thrust of the boy's jaw and his clenched fists.

She touched the windowpane, anticipating disaster.

At last the boy swung around and started across the parking lot toward the center. Cat watched him approach, aware of his furious countenance and his fast stride. He'd covered half of the lot when the red-haired teenager slammed out of the Camaro and sprinted after him. In the same split second that Cat wondered why the boy didn't turn, she realized that the teenagers' shouts were drowning out the sound of their friend's pursuit. The boy couldn't hear him!

Cat pounded on the window and called to him. "Behind you!"

The boy's head snapped up and he halted, confused.

"Turn!" Cat screamed.

The boy swung around defensively and collided with the advancing teenager, driving a shoulder into his chest. The much-larger boy looked shocked. He obviously hadn't expected his quarry to turn. He swayed in a state of suspended animation for a moment, then staggered backward, lost his balance on a loose rock, and sat down, hard.

Cat suppressed a chuckle. It had looked accidental, but whether it had actually been premeditated or not, it was a darn effective move. Even the rowdy kids in the car were stunned into silence.

She wanted to applaud, but the dark-haired boy's triumph was short-lived. The carload of teenagers started in on him again almost immediately, spewing insults and jeers. "Slime!" one of them screamed. "West End scum!"

The bay window shook as the boy stormed inside the center and slammed the door. Cat held her breath as he whirled around, furious. Was he angry at her for intervening? She saw the glitter of tears in his eyes and knew he was more than angry, he was enraged, at her, at them, at the planet and everyone on it.

She knew that look, and it tore at her heart. She understood the fury, the bewilderment, even the loneliness. His eyes held all the despair of a rebel who didn't know how to end the war—with himself, with the system. Cat had learned some things during her difficult childhood. When you lived on the wrong side of the tracks, anger was a given. When you lived on the wrong side of the law, it became an impenetrable shield. It separated you from everything that was nourishing and loving and life-giving.

She knew this boy. She *was* this boy.

He came to the window to check out the situation on the street, and Cat moved out of his way. Observing him silently, she realized that he was older than she'd first thought, perhaps even fourteen or fifteen. His stature was small, but his boyish features were as inured to hardship as any back-alley transient's.

Once he'd assured himself that the Camaro and all its occupants were gone, he glanced at Cat, a jerky, suspicious movement that revealed a gut-punch of vulnerability. It made Cat inexpressibly sad for him.

"Are you all right?" she asked.

He shrugged, and finally she remembered that she had a crumbled bag of cheese puffs in her pocket. She produced the bag and held it out to him. "Ackerman's?"

He didn't take any, but he looked for a minute as though he might. Encouraged, Cat took her overture a step further. "Were you *trying* to knock that guy on his butt?" she asked softly.

The grimace he made must have been meant to be terrifying. His brows furrowed and his mouth screwed up. But she could see the twitch of pride in his jaw, the half-twist of a smile in his eyes. That was when she knew she could work with him. That was when she knew she had to work with him.

"What's your name?" she asked.

The back door slammed before he could answer, and a moment later Gwen entered the room carrying a box of supplies. "Johnny?" she said, setting her load down on the table. "What are you doing here today? Is something wrong?"

"Nah," he said, "I been thinking about the Sinclair trial is all. I'm not so sure I want to testify."

By Gwen's expression, Cat knew something *was* wrong.

Gwen asked Johnny to wait for her in her office, and as soon as he'd gone, she turned at once to Cat. "Did something happen? Did he say anything to you?"

Cat described the incident outside, and Gwen shook her head in despair. "Johnny's the key witness in an assault case against the son of a prominent family. The pressure on him not to testify has been pretty intense." She drew in a breath. "I want him to do it, Cat. Just once he needs to know what it feels like to be a good citizen."

Cat touched Gwen's arm reassuringly. Her friend's

consternation was so apparent that it reminded Cat why she'd chosen to work with troubled children. She wanted passionately to help teenagers like Johnny avoid the pain she'd been through. And to have a chance at some of the opportunities she'd missed early on. It was one of the promises she'd made herself during her ordeal in Purdy Hall. It was more than a career goal, it was a calling.

"Gwen, has anyone been assigned to work with Johnny yet?"

"Not officially. I'm seeing him until one of the other counselors has an open spot in their schedule."

Cat's voice was urgent. "Let me work with him. Okay, Gwen? I know I can get through to him." Cat steeled herself for rejection. She certainly hadn't demonstrated any ability to help anyone so far that day, including herself. But Gwen's response was a faint smile.

Cat reacted immediately. "So . . . what are you saying? I can?"

"Not so fast." Gwen cocked an eyebrow skeptically, as though to let her hasty young protégé know she had no intention of giving in too easily. "It did occur to me that you and Johnny have a lot in common," she said. "Then again, you do have a tendency to fly off the handle. We both know that wouldn't be appropriate role-modeling for a boy like him."

Cat raised her right hand. "No flying off the handle. No flying anywhere!"

The faint smile reemerged. "I suppose it might work—if it's all right with Johnny."

Cat actually had a lump in her throat. "Thank you."

"Do a good job," Gwen said softly. She started for her office, hesitated, and swung around. "Wait a minute—you do know who your new client is, don't you?"

"Sure, Johnny . . . something."

Gwen's face lost its color. "I think maybe you'd better sit down, dear. His name is Johnny Drescher, and he happens to be Blake Wheeler's star witness."

"Oh, Gwen, no—" Cat pressed her fingers to her lips and turned away. There were jokes, and then there were cruel jokes.

From behind her, Gwen's voice was suddenly stern. "Listen to me, Cat. If you're going to back out, then do it now, before I go tell Johnny. And if you're not, then you'd better start rigging yourself for heavy weather, because you and your new client have an appointment with Mr. Wheeler at ten A.M. Wednesday morning."

On the same afternoon that Cat D'Angelo was acquiring her first client, Blake Wheeler was losing a tennis match to Sam Delahunt, the mayor of Cameron Bay. Blake knew his timing had been off throughout the last couple of games. He just wasn't sure why. When it came to athletics, he was a man obsessed. Murder trials and grand jury hearings came and went, but nothing interfered with his tennis game. Sports were his safety valve, his escape from the pressure cooker.

"Fifteen-thirty," Blake called out as he tossed the ball into the air and stretched to smash it. Unleashing the coiled strength in his muscles, he willed his body to execute a perfect serve. *Ace,* he commanded silently as taut catgut *sponged* against Day-Glo orange fuzz.

But Blake didn't get his ace. He didn't even get the ball in the court. Somewhere between the mental command and the physical execution, a strange and lovely vision short-circuited his concentration.

Staring up into a pale aureole of dazzling sunshine, Blake blinked and thought he saw a woman's hand drift in front of his eyes. Delicately boned and erotically graceful, it seemed to reach out to him and stroke the air currents. Cherry-red nails shimmered in the sunlight as the hand rolled onto its back, and the slender index finger curled in a sexy invitation. Come hither, the beckoning finger was saying.

Blake grimaced in disbelief. The last impression he had as he arced toward the tennis ball above his head was of those tapering red fingernails. They made a man think about erotic couplings in shuttered rooms. They were the kind of nails that tangled wantonly in a man's hair and left passionate marks on his back. Where the hell had they come from?

When Blake came to an instant later, the tennis ball was wafting over Sam Delahunt's head.

"You playing baseball, son?" Sam called to him.

Blake touched a finger to his tongue and held it up. "Wind's at my back," he said, straight-faced. He dropped the next serve right in the middle of the mayor's court. As the puffing, portly man lobbed the ball back to him, Blake stepped into the easy backhand return. Unfortunately, the phantom vision chose that moment to strike again. This time Blake saw glittery dark eyes and sweet, cherry-red lips. As the lips parted slightly and breathed his name, he popped the ball over the ten-foot netting that separated the courts. It landed in a birdbath.

"Hole in one," Sam hooted.

Blake barely registered Sam's gibe. He raked a hand through his hair, perplexed. He wasn't a believer in visions, but this one had a name: Cat D'Angelo. It was the details that confused him. She hadn't been wearing red nail polish that morning. Or red lipstick. He would have remembered!

"Service!" Sam shouted.

Mercifully the match was over after the next short volley.

"You been practicing again, son?" Sam asked, chortling as he lumbered over to shake Blake's hand. "Sure was an interesting game of tennis."

"Tennis?" Blake muttered. "That was Nerf ball."

"Come on along." Sam slapped him soundly across the shoulder blades. "I think you need a drink more than I do."

Seated in the country club's lounge bar, the two

men drank tall Scotches on the rocks while Sam expounded at length on Blake's brilliant future. "Damn, but I wish I was your age again, boy," he confessed, pride and envy in his voice. "You've got the world right smack in the palm of your hand if you want it. You know that, don't you? You can be governor. Hell, you can be president if you want." He lifted his glass and toasted Blake. "The right people are lining up behind us, Blake. And they've got big plans for you."

Blake acknowledged Sam with a nod. He'd heard this pep talk before, and it always brought to mind the things he disliked most about the political arena— the power games, the horse-trading, and influence peddling. Blake understood the machinery, and the kind of grease it took to keep the gears meshing, but he didn't involve himself in maintenance work any more than was absolutely necessary. He left the tune-ups and lube jobs to Sam and the professional politicians.

Blake also knew what was coming next. Sam wasn't merely his primary supporter, he was also his ex-father-in-law. Sam's interest in getting Blake elected governor someday ranked only slightly higher than his interest in getting Blake and his daughter back together. Luckily, Linda Delahunt, the ex-wife in question, knew exactly how foolish that would be. Linda had a thriving career of her own in the public defender's office, but neither she nor Blake had been able to convince Sam that they weren't the perfect "first couple."

As it turned out, Sam surprised Blake. It wasn't Linda on his mind at all. It was an assault and battery case Blake had pending.

"I suppose you know the Sinclairs are pretty worried about that oldest boy of theirs," he said conversationally. "What's his name? Skip?"

Blake bit through a melting ice cube and swallowed the cool, slippery pieces. "They should be,

Sam. Skip beat up a transient. Just for kicks, apparently."

"I heard the old guy was a bum, Blake, a wino."

"Is that a reason to dislocate a sixty-year-old man's jaw and crack three of his ribs?"

"Skip says the man tried to rob him."

"There's a witness who says there was no robbery and no attempt. He says the attack was unprovoked."

Sam drained his drink and held the glass up, a signal for the bartender to bring him another. "Yes, well, that's just what I wanted to talk to you about, Blake. That young witness of yours, Johnny Drescher. I hear he's a bad sort."

"What are you getting at, Sam?"

"I think you know, son. The Sinclairs are a fine family. Why, they sit on the school board and the arts council. I don't have to tell you it would be real hard on them if their son was convicted of assault based on evidence from an unreliable witness."

Blake did know what Sam was getting at, and it had less to do with the Sinclairs being a fine family than with their being major financial supporters of Sam's last campaign. It was understood that their support would extend to any future campaign of Blake's as well, of course. Yes, Blake knew what Sam was after. Nothing unethical, nothing illegal, just some special consideration for Skip Sinclair.

Blake considered his longtime friend and ally. "Who said Johnny was unreliable?" Blake asked.

Sam took a long swallow of the drink the bartender had just brought him. "Well, what else could he be, Blake? Been in and out of Purdy Hall, I hear, and on probation more often than not. A real troublemaker . . ."

Blake nodded as Sam continued, but he was only half listening. His thoughts had drifted back to Sam's earlier reference to the reformatory, and in his mind he was interrogating a sixteen-year-old defendant in a pretrial hearing. Like so many kids her age, she'd armored herself with attitude, a flip manner and a smart mouth. But underneath he'd sensed fear, even terror. He'd never understood why she hadn't cracked. Most kids her age would have surrendered to the fear and seized the opportunity to save themselves. She hadn't.

He fingered his glass, and through its steamy condensation, he watched the remaining ice cubes melt. Questions took shape in his mind. Who was the woman he'd encountered at the youth center that morning? A defiant and terrified child? Or the phantom who'd invaded his visual field on the tennis court: the woman with long red fingernails and a trace of sadness in her mouth.

Sam stared down his ample nose at Blake. "You're kinda quiet today, son. Seem restless, a little twitchy even. You got something on your mind?"

Blake had something on his mind, all right. He was caught up in a strange awareness, a realization that certain explosive events in the past were never completed, never finished and filed away. They had an emotional half-life all their own, an unresolved energy. They lived on a continuum that looped back in on the present and became the future.

Cat D'Angelo was just that, he realized. An explosion. She was a long red stick of dynamite that the past had conjured up and dropped right in his lap.

Three

Blake Wheeler skipped up the short flight of cement steps to the youth center's front door, Johnny Drescher's file tucked under his arm. He knew Gwen wouldn't be expecting him to return the file the day after he'd picked it up, but he needed a plausible excuse for dropping by. Crimson fingernails, shuttered rooms, and passion had colored his dreams last night. The visions were beginning to haunt him.

With any luck, he thought, entering the reception area, he would flush out Cat D'Angelo without arousing any undue attention. The reception room was unusually quiet, no clients waiting, no smiling secretary at the front desk. It was early yet, he realized, checking his watch, not even nine A.M. All of the offices stood open but one. He was pondering the possibility that it might be her office when the door swung open and Cat wandered out. Bingo!

Unaware of him, she walked to the water cooler, poured herself a cup, and then whirled as though someone had whispered in her ear that he was there. It was amazing how quickly she wiped the astonishment from her face.

"What brings you back so soon?" she asked.

She was suddenly bright-eyed, suddenly unfailingly polite, as though he were the UPS man or some kid selling magazine subscriptions. An act, he thought. She's dissembling like crazy, but why the burning need to pretend with me?

"The Drescher file," he said. "I'm through with it."

"And so quickly."

She eyed the file. Blake waited for her to reach for it and was secretly amused when she didn't. It was obvious she had no intention of playing his waiting game today. "We've got a meeting tomorrow, according to Gwen," he explained. "I like to be prepared."

"A meeting— Yes, so we do." Cat set down the water cup. She'd nearly crushed it in her surprise at seeing him, and even now, with her nerves sparking like the touch of positive and negative wires, she didn't trust herself not to spill it.

"Is tomorrow going to give you enough time?" Blake asked. "Gwen said you were taking over the case."

Cat drew in a breath, bathing her nerves in oxygen. "I don't anticipate any problems." Right up there with the biggest whoppers of my life, she thought. She anticipated nothing *but* problems. She hadn't even met with Johnny officially yet. They had an extended session scheduled for later that morning. If she couldn't convince the boy to testify, there wouldn't be any meeting with Blake Wheeler. Talk about winding up with egg on her face!

"Where are you staying?" Blake asked conversationally. "At your folk's old place?"

"No—" A sagging white clapboard house flashed into Cat's mind. The place would be empty now that Mary D'Angelo, Cat's mother, had gone back to Arkansas to nurse her own ailing mother. Empty and yet filled with memories. Cat doubted if she could even bring herself to visit her childhood home.

"I'm staying at the Kirkpatricks'," she said, smiling to cover her abruptness. "It's a couple of blocks from here. Gwen arranged for me to house-sit while they're in Mexico."

"Yes, I know the place." He voiced the comment

casually, letting his eyes drift over her features, hesitating on her mouth for a moment, then searching the hand she'd raised to her lapel. "You didn't have red nail polish on yesterday, did you?"

"Red nail polish?"

His gaze shimmered with quicksilver. And his smile. There was something unnervingly sensual in the faint curve of his lips. Why in the world had he asked her a question like that? "I never wear nail polish," she insisted, holding out naturally buffed nails to prove it.

"Shame."

"Is there something wrong with my nails?"

"No, they're beautiful. They're just not red."

Beautiful? That word might have thrown her if it hadn't been for the odd inflections in his voice. He sounded amused, aroused, and faintly disappointed. Cat stiffened. Perhaps it was old-fashioned, but she still equated red nails with wild parties and fast women. "What's your point, Mr. Wheeler?"

"I don't think anybody will mind if you call me Blake."

She flushed slightly. *What in the world is he up to?* "I really think we should keep it professional, don't you?"

"Not necessarily." Blake watched the sparks fly in her eyes and decided it was going to be a damn interesting meeting tomorrow, red nails or not. "But if professional works for you," he added, "I can live with it."

Cat worked at the button cuff of her sleeve, tightening it around her wrist a notch. Oh, yes, this was the Blake Wheeler she remembered. Forever keeping his opponents off balance, baiting, probing for the fatal chink in the armor. Even with sixteen-year-old girls. There's just one flaw in that approach, *Mr. Wheeler*, she thought, raising her head to meet his riveting gaze full on. *Catherine D'Angelo isn't sixteen anymore.*

* * *

"Tough guy, huh?"

Johnny Drescher slouched low in his chair and kicked aimlessly at the leg of Cat's desk. "Tough enough," he replied.

Cat clicked her fingernails along her desktop in a faint drum roll, unable to completely curb her frustration. She'd been trying for the best part of the morning to get Johnny to open up and tell her why he'd changed his mind about testifying. She knew he'd been frightened off by the harassment, but if she suggested that, he would probably deny it.

It looked as though she was going to have to call Wheeler and cancel their meeting tomorrow, a task she didn't relish. Still, her relationship with Johnny was far more important than one meeting. As she absently tapped the desk and contemplated the boy's slumped posture, an idea struck.

"That red-haired kid you decked yesterday afternoon," she said, casually settling back in her chair. "Who was he?"

Johnny shrugged without looking up. "Skip Sinclair."

"Sinclair? The boy who assaulted the transient?"

"Yeah, that was Skip."

So that's how it was. "Skip, yes, that's right." She kept her voice conversational. "I hear he's a varsity letterman at Bayside High. Clean-cut kid, nice family, no priors."

Johnny glared at her suspiciously.

Cat was going partly on what she knew about the case from Gwen and partly on pure bluff. She just hoped Johnny wasn't a fan of old detective movies, because the strategy she had in mind was one of Sam Spade's favorites.

"Skip says it didn't happen the way you tell it, Johnny. Or that's what I heard anyway." Her voice took on an edge. "He says the old man was drunk and tried to rob him. Skip says *he* was the victim, and the old man should go to jail—"

"Skip's a stinkin' liar."

"That's what he says about you."

Johnny sprang from the chair. "He's a *liar*! That old man wasn't trying to rob anybody! Skip broke his jaw for the hell of it. He was laughing and bragging about it!" Johnny spun away and punched the air violently.

Galvanized, Cat stood. "Don't let him get away with it, Johnny." She spoke softly to his rigid back. "Johnny—"

He half-turned. "What?"

"You're the only chance the old man's got."

She could see the warring emotions in his features. He was afraid of Skip Sinclair, but he probably despised him too—for beating up a defenseless old man. Bullies like Sinclair had many enemies, but very few with the courage to take a stand against them.

Cat pressed on, her heart thudding. "Nobody saw it happen but you, Johnny. If you don't testify, they'll prosecute the old man, and Skip will get off. They'll believe Skip, dammit. They'll believe his version of what happened, and he knows it! Don't let him get away with that."

Johnny pivoted and started for the door.

Cat's heart sank. "Tomorrow at ten, the courthouse!" she called after him. She rushed out of her office just as he reached the center's front door. "I'll be there too," she promised him as he yanked the door open.

He disappeared from sight, and she slumped against the doorframe, exhausted and wondering what she'd done wrong. She had been so sure she could reach him.

She was still in her doorway when Gwen came out of her office a few minutes later.

"Rough session?" Gwen asked.

"Dismal." Cat gave her a brief rundown.

Gwen's sympathetic smile held traces of irony. "Hang in there, kid," she advised. "Remember what you were like at his age?" She walked to the coat tree by the front door, whisked off Cat's cable-knit sweater, and held it up. "Sounds to me like you did all you could under the circumstances. Now why don't you go on home. You don't have anything else this afternoon, and you've got a big day tomorrow."

"*If* Johnny shows up for the meeting."

Gwen tossed her the sweater. "If Johnny doesn't show up, you and Mr. Wheeler can talk strategy. Between the two of you—mature professionals that you both are—I'm sure you'll figure out a way to rein in one recalcitrant teenager." She winked, then couldn't suppress a smile. "In the meantime," she added, "do something fun. Take your mind off this mess for a while."

Cat was sure nothing had been invented that could take her mind off the current mess. She also saw no immediate reason to meet with Blake Wheeler if Johnny wasn't going to be there. And several reasons not to! But she slipped on her sweater like a mature professional. It was only as she breezed past Gwen and reached the front door that she turned and made a face at her friend's back. So much for maturity.

The green cat's-eye shooter bounced along the hard-packed dirt, its trajectory the only remaining marble in the chalked circle.

"Yeoww! She's a deadeye!"

As the shooter hit its mark and knocked the marble over the line, Cat settled back on her haunches, grabbed her knees, and smiled. She hadn't lost her stuff. Her rival players, two West End boys who looked to be about nine and five, respectively, jerked their heads toward her. The five-year-old's eyes were wide with astonishment.

The older boy, Biff, regarded her suspiciously. "How'd you get so good?" he asked.

Cat snapped her thumb off her index finger. "Got

the touch," she said, unable to resist ragging him a little.

"She's got the touch, Biff," the young boy whispered.

"Hmmmph," was Biff's succinct comment. With that, he began gathering up his marbles to leave. He knew when he was outmatched, and he wasn't going to hang around and gawk at his competitor. Dropping the last marble into his black felt drawstring bag, he cuffed the younger boy, who finally dragged his worshipful gaze from Cat and followed his haughty mentor off down the sidewalk.

The little guy turned back once, grinning broadly as Cat winked. Cat laughed softly and let herself fall back on a strip of cool grass in the shade of a huge maple tree. The whole neighborhood would soon know about the strange lady who was house-sitting the Kirkpatricks' place. At least the fiercely competitive game of "potsie" had taken her mind off the session with Blake Wheeler tomorrow. Now if she could just keep her mind off—

Cat hadn't even completed the thought before his features materialized: the lion-gold hair and dark brows, the deep tan defined by jutting facial bones. "Matinee-idol handsome," one telejournalist had gushed.

He's not *that* handsome, Cat thought, but her stomach tightened as his smile danced in her mind—faintly amused, sexy as sin. Small wonder she'd once fixed her adolescent dreams on the golden boy of Cameron Bay. One-sided as that infatuation had been, she reminded herself sharply.

Her stomach was churning by the time she rolled to her side and locked her attention on the first thing she saw: the Kirkpatricks' wood-shake cottage with its dormered windows and snow-white shutters. The retired couple's cozy cottage and small fenced yard were nearly lost in a riotous profusion of crimson rhododendrons and lavender lilacs. The bucolic charm of it soothed Cat momentarily, but the meeting with Wheeler popped into her head again as she rose to go in for dinner. Maybe the encounter kept haunting her because she hadn't psyched herself up for it.

"Good morning, Mr. Wheeler," she said, smiling brightly at her reflection in the mirrored clock in the entry hall. Not mature enough, she decided, trying it again as she entered the kitchen and headed for the refrigerator.

"How are you this morning, Mr. Wheeler?" With a brisk nod she opened the refrigerator door and perused the contents. "You already know my client, of course—Johnny Drescher."

She loaded up with vegetables from the crisper for a quick salad and walked to the sink to rinse them. "I'm sure we're going to make great headway, the three of us. We're all interested in seeing justice done, so with that in mind—and in the spirit of cooperation—let's proceed."

Laying it on a bit thick, she decided, but she was determined to make an impression. There would be no angry outbursts, no failures of nerve. She was going to prove to all of them—to herself, to Gwen, and especially to Wheeler—that she could handle anything he had to dish out. Anytime, anywhere.

Moments later, standing at the sink and absently munching on a carrot stick, she said a little prayer that Johnny would show up. For both their sakes, but mostly for Johnny's. She would be there to provide support for him, and to see that he wasn't compromised in any way. As an eyewitness to the crime, he didn't need a lawyer, but he did need an advocate, someone to look out for his interests during the long ordeal of the trial. Whisking a gleaming knife from its sharpener-holder, she began chopping vegetables with quick, decisive strokes. No one would railroad her client the way she'd been railroaded. Her hand slowed as she thought about the escalating sequence of disasters that had preceded her trial, quite possibly the worst of which was a meeting with Wheeler much like the one scheduled for tomorrow.

What would his office be like now that he was the district attorney? she wondered. She remembered a smallish room, a glass-top desk, and slatted light filtering through half-closed venetian blinds. It was hot in that room, close and sultry with the summer sun beating against the window . . . and he was angry . . . soft eyes, beautiful dove-gray eyes, the low rush of his breath.

Her breathing faltered, and the knife nearly slipped from her grasp. She remembered too well, too much.

She knew she should be dealing with it, here and now, before she faced him again tomorrow. She had to come to terms with what had happened at that meeting. With what he'd done. And what *she'd* done. Since that day she must have asked herself a thousand times why she'd behaved like such a shameless little idiot.

A sharp rap at the door startled her out of her reverie. She dropped the knife, her heart jolting wildly. By the time she had herself under control, she was already in the living room, scrutinizing the silent door. Had she imagined the knock? Had whoever it was gone? The only person she could imagine paying an impromptu visit was Gwen. Or Johnny, perhaps.

Suddenly she felt foolish staring at a doorknob. She slapped damp palms against her jeans and got on with acting like a mature adult.

The rosy-pink glare of the setting sun blinded her for a moment as the door swung wide. Even when her vision cleared she couldn't discern anyone in the pearlescent haze of light. Then she realized she was looking for someone tall, someone as tall as Blake Wheeler—

"Hi."

The voice came from below her eye level. It was soft and shy, and Catherine immediately looked down. The cornflower-blue eyes staring up at her belonged to her favorite competitor at marbles. Watch out, all five-year-old girls, she thought. This one's going to be a lady-killer in about ten years. "Hi," she said, "you're Biff's friend. What's your name?"

He pursed his lips and lifted both shoulders. "Name's Bumper. Sure wish I could shoot marbles like you."

"Oh . . . you do?" She crouched to smile at him. She never could resist a shy man. "You can. You just need someone to show you how. Would you like me to?"

"Okay."

He was so adorably serious her heart twisted. She touched his nose and laughed to soften the graininess in her throat. "It's kind of late tonight. How about this weekend?"

He took a step backward, nodding vigorously. After a couple more steps he suddenly stopped. "What's *your* name, lady?"

"Catherine."

"Caff . . . Caffrun?"

A smile broke on her face and her heart tilted oddly. "You can call me Cat."

Blake Wheeler stood at the window of his fourth-floor courthouse office and watched the Mustang glide to the curb and stop. The crimson car was made wine red by the purple cast of his tinted windows. The dark-haired woman who slid out from behind the steering wheel and smoothed her clothes was more exotic than he remembered. He glanced at his watch. Five minutes before ten exactly. Why didn't it surprise him that she was right on time?

She walked around the car to the sidewalk, breezed up the first tier of steps, and stopped at the glossy marble monument that dominated the building's facade. She seemed to be checking out her appearance in its planed surface, and that possibility made him smile.

You're perfect, he told her silently. From the shiny coil of your immaculate French knot to the smooth calf pumps on your feet, you're perfect. His eyes did another quick pass up her body, and an impulse sparked in his groin as he thought about unleashing her tight knot of hair. A man would have to be in a coma or dead not to want to free all that wild, dark abundance.

Recalling the tempestuous sixteen-year-old girl in his office so many years ago, Blake compared her precocious sexuality to this woman's. It was no contest. The sixteen-year-old had thrown him some curves, but this woman galvanized him. The girl had flaunted her sensuality. The woman was trying her damnedest to hide hers. But she wasn't succeeding, not by any stretch. Her attempts accentuated every riveting detail, from the prim navy skirt that revealed a show girl's sleek legs to her smoky-black eyes and the intriguing width of her mouth. The more she consciously restrained her natural eroticism, the more she unconsciously excited the imagination. Catherine D'Angelo presented a virtual feast for the male imagination, and at the moment, his was going wild.

Watching her walk toward the entrance, he felt the hair on his arms prick as though he'd entered an electrical field. Some women were a stimulant to the senses; she was a current of static electricity. She made muscles jump everywhere you'd expect a man's muscles to jump and some places you wouldn't, like his heart. "There's a new experience for you, Wheeler," he thought aloud, irony in his lowered voice. "Your heart. It still works."

He allowed himself one last look before he got back down to business. And in that last penetrating glance, he saw her curl her thumb into her right index finger and make a snapping gesture, almost as though she were flicking away some unwanted bit of debris.

Now what was that all about? he wondered.

• • •

"I'll let Mr. Wheeler know you're here, Ms. D'Angelo."
Blake Wheeler's secretary was a pleasant-looking
woman in her forties with tortoiseshell glasses and
an industrious air.

At least he had the sense to hire someone effi-
cient, Cat observed, nodding politely. As the secretary buzzed Wheeler, Cat glanced into the adjoining
waiting room to see if Johnny had arrived. There
was no sign of him, but she did not let it ruffle her
composure. She had made up her mind that even if
the teenager didn't show up, the meeting with
Wheeler was going to go fine. Just fine. She'd been
coaching herself all morning, building her confidence to a fare-thee-well.

Still, Cat wasn't quite prepared for the secretary
to bustle immediately to Blake's door and open it.
Perhaps she'd expected to be kept waiting. Mentally
squaring her shoulders, she entered and paused as
the door shut firmly behind her. Blake was standing
by the window, his arms folded as though he'd been
waiting there for some time.

For her? If it took her a second to get her bearings, she didn't let the wobble show. Putting all
hesitation out of her mind, she walked straight to
him, her hand extended.

He didn't unfold his arms immediately. Instead,
he smiled at her in an offhand, intrigued sort of
way, and in the process he created a disquieting
intimacy with his eyes. His expression said, What's
with you, lady? What makes Cat D'Angelo run? It
also said he would take his own sweet time finding
out.

He's done it again, she realized, glancing at her
hand. She was hanging out in space like a complete
idiot. All right, she thought, irritation flaring, be
that way. Be a calculating bastard and see how far it
gets you. With no preamble whatsoever she wrested
one of his hands free and shook it vigorously. "Good

morning," she said, not caring in the least that it was his left hand she'd hijacked.

"Hi," he said, adding in the next breath, "Good morning."

If she'd surprised him, he only revealed it with the faint huskiness in his voice.

He moved deftly to bring their right hands together and to still her quickness with a slow, firm handshake. "I've been looking forward to this," he said. In the light his eyes were the same glinting silver she remembered. Hard steel. Dove soft. Whatever he wanted them to be.

She disengaged from him, but the warm imprint of his palm remained on her skin. Warm hands, cold heart, was that how it worked? Or did Blake Wheeler even own a heart? Allowing herself that one last mental knife thrust, she chose the wing chair that sat to the right of his desk and seated herself.

Blake watched her taut, precise movements as she crossed her show-girl's legs and adjusted her skirt, and the one crazy thought that invaded his mind, the *only* thought was: How do I get you alone somewhere, lady? How do I get you alone?

It didn't surprise him at all, that hot, quick impulse. He'd felt it coming from the moment he saw her step out of her car. Now the urge was playing itself out physically, running sweet and wild down his body like a riff of hard-rock guitar music. The cascading beat aroused muscles clear to his groin.

"Johnny Drescher will be here soon," she informed him, looking up as she finished with her skirt.

He didn't doubt it. At the moment he couldn't imagine any male not giving her whatever she wanted, Johnny Drescher included.

"I thought we'd . . . talk strategy," she said.

"Sure. What sort of strategy?" He sat on the window ledge and folded his arms.

"Well, Johnny's ambivalent about testifying, so first I'd like to put him at ease. Maybe we could talk about something other than the trial? I know your time is limited, but he takes a little warming up."

Oh, lady, be careful feeding me lines like that, he thought, or I'm going to be dangerous. "I've got all the time you want," he said, aware that his biceps had contracted beneath his hands. Hard time, crying time, anything your heart desires, Catherine, Cat . . . *lady.*

He almost chuckled as she pulled a notepad from her purse and flipped it open to a long list of numbered items. She didn't seem to have a clue what she was doing to him with her long-stemmed legs and her wide, sensual mouth.

"He likes the Seattle Seahawks," she said, consulting her list, "and Eddie Murphy movies. Did you happen to see *Beverly Hills Cop?*"

"The original or the sequel?"

"Uh . . . the original."

He smiled. "Three times. I could discuss it scene by scene, blow by blow with Johnny, if you think that would help."

She glanced up at him in surprise, as though she hadn't expected his cooperation. "Yes, I think that would help." A smile softened her mouth. "Three times? I never thought of you as going to movies."

"I wasn't aware you'd been thinking about me."

She flushed slightly, and he rescued her with a quick shrug. He didn't want her defensive today. No, he didn't want that at all. "I love a good movie, Cat— Sorry, Catherine."

Her color deepened. "It's all right," she said finally. "Cat, I mean."

"Cat, then." He liked the feel of her name in his mouth, and the way it resonated low in his throat. "I love a lot of things that might surprise you." What Blake loved at the moment was the way her eyes searched him, as though she wasn't quite sure who Blake Wheeler was. She was charming in her uncertainty. The office window's purple aura lent her gaze a beguiling fragility.

"Anything else?" he asked, referring to her concern about Johnny. "Anything at all, I mean it."

She stared down at the list in her hand, smiling, and then her expression took on a sadness. It was a soft, erotic shade of beauty he hadn't seen in her before—or in any woman. It was like a glimpse into a secret garden. All he had offered was his time, a helping hand, but she was responding, almost involuntarily it seemed, to his simple gesture. Was she always sad when someone did something kind for her? Was she so unused to it?

"Are you all right?" he asked.

"Yes . . . fine. I just never expected—" She wet her lips, as though confused, even shaken.

Watching her struggle for control, Blake felt a tightening in his body, a quickening in his mind. Somewhere in his awareness a veil parted. In that revealing glimpse he had discovered the key to Cat D'Angelo's secret nature. He had seen the depth of her vulnerability. A kind word, a gentle touch, and her defenses would thaw and bleed like spring snow. She would cry softly and open her heart to the man who could touch that sadness within her. She would give him anything, whatever he wanted. She would bond with him emotionally, fuse with him physically like tears fuse when they touch, like fire consumes.

When Blake spoke, the words were tempered, husky. "What was it you didn't expect, Cat? Help from a guy like me?"

"No . . . it wasn't that."

The hesitation in her voice told Blake it *was* that. Precious secrets were contained in her soft, sad expression; in the notebook clutched in her hand. And in her unwillingness to look up at him. She was beautiful and complicated and angry, but she was also wounded. The man who knew that would have incredible power over her. The power to hurt, he realized, the power to *heal* . . .

The last word pierced Blake softly. It resonated in his mind and jolted him with an emotion he didn't recognize. His jaw tightened, oddly hot and tender. For an instant, just a fraction of a heartbeat, he was out of control. He wanted to touch her, a crazy impulse, but he could almost feel the pain of it.

"Cat—"

She glanced up, startled, perhaps by the low force in his voice. Her eyes were suddenly wary, and she stiffened in the chair.

The desire to touch her was swift and sharp. And yet Blake could see that this was not the vulnerable woman of seconds before. He locked off the impulse with a massive flex of will, walling it up somewhere in the reaches of his consciousness. Blood surged, warm in his veins, and he felt the pulsing heat of it, the power. It was control that Blake Wheeler understood. It was controlling power.

"What is it?" she asked.

He shook the question off. "A thought about the Seahawk's last game. I'll save it for Johnny."

Her reaction had jolted Blake into an awareness. Acting on his desires with a woman like Cat D'Angelo would be like playing with a lighted stick of dynamite. For all her hidden sadness, she wasn't the kind of woman who aroused gentleness in men. She carried too much pride in her eyes, too much fire and fight. She aroused carnal instincts and hot flashes of desire. Like red wine, she heated the blood and loosened the inhibitions. She was the danger zone. Beyond that, she was too busy protecting her wounds to know what she needed from a man, and most men wouldn't have a clue how to give it to her if she did.

But Blake knew. *He knew just how to touch her, just how to reach her tender heart and move her to tears* . . .

The notebook slipped from her hand, and that's when he realized that she was still watching him, staring up at him with all the bewilderment of a cornered animal. The soft, startled sound in her throat told him he'd been stalking her visually, hunting her down with his eyes.

"What is it?" she asked.

From somewhere he found the presence of mind to defuse the situation. "Nothing—sorry. It's that thing you're doing with your hands. Does it mean something?"

They both stared at her right hand, at the sprung thumb and coiled forefinger. The sound she made was husky, surprised, like laughter. "I didn't know I was doing it," she said.

"Doing what?"

Her thumb flicked automatically. "I shoot marbles."

The door banged open behind them, and the secretary entered in a rush. "Mr. Wheeler, excuse me. There's a young man—"

She never got to finish her introduction. Johnny Drescher pushed past her, bringing with him a gust of turbulence to the already charged atmosphere. He had on torn jeans, a red bandanna around his head, and a stormy expression on his face. He looked wild, a teenager from hell, but Cat had never been so glad to see anyone in her life.

Four

"Johnny—" Cat was out of her chair instantly. "Is something wrong?"

The boy shook his head and adjusted his worn leather jacket aggressively, checking out the office as he did so. "Let's get this over with," was all he said.

"You're going to testify?" Both Cat and Blake spoke at once, and the chorus of their voices sounded too eager, Cat realized. She waited for Johnny's reaction.

"I haven't made up my mind yet," the boy said, studying Blake with undisguised distrust. "What do you want from me, anyway?"

Blake walked to his desk and sat down. He motioned for Cat and Johnny to do the same, at which point Johnny shuffled to the back wall instead and remained standing. Cat looked from the man to the rebellious boy with the uneasy sense of having to choose sides. After a moment she joined Johnny.

Blake acknowledged them both with a nod, as though he regularly interviewed hostile teenagers flanked by their designated counselor-bodyguards.

"How are you, Johnny?" he said, smiling.

Cat remained silent, admiring Blake's style as he attempted to engage the boy in small talk about action movies. His tone was easy and conspiratorial, man-to-man stuff. Nearly irresistible to the rest of the human race, she supposed, but it wasn't washing with Johnny. The teenager was having none of the buddy-buddy approach, at least not that day.

Cat wasn't surprised when Blake threw in the towel and moved on to the point of the interview, pressing Johnny to tell him everything he knew about the Sinclair assault case. She *was* surprised when Johnny complied. Blake jotted notes on a pad as Johnny recounted what he'd seen.

"Where did the fight take place?" Blake asked finally.

Johnny adjusted his jacket nervously, opening and closing the elaborate zipper. "It wasn't a fight. The old man was trying to bum some money from Sinclair was all."

"But you did see who started it?"

"I told you, it wasn't a fight," Johnny said. "The old man was drunk or something. He couldn't have fought his way out of a wet paper bag. Sinclair went after him, attacked him for no reason."

Cat glanced from Johnny to Blake. The teenager was visibly uneasy, and giving off signals of increasing agitation, but Blake hadn't seemed to notice.

Thoughtful, Blake leaned back in his chair and studied the boy. "You're sure. The other man didn't provoke him, call him names . . . ?"

Johnny shook his head.

"Did the old man have a weapon?"

Another headshake, more emphatic this time.

"Give it a minute, Johnny, think about it. You didn't see him pull a knife and demand money from Skip?"

"No!"

Cat stifled the urge to intervene. Blake was going at it all wrong. Even the tone of his voice implied that he was questioning the truth of Johnny's story. She didn't understand why he was taking a confrontational approach, especially since she'd warned him that Johnny would be difficult.

With some effort she remained silent through the next several questions, and finally Blake ended his interrogation.

"If you have any doubts about what you saw," he told the boy, "or about your testimony, now's the time to tell me."

When the teenager didn't answer, Blake dropped a bomb. "Perjury carries a stiff penalty, Johnny."

The boy jerked savagely at the zipper of his jacket.

Cat's throat tightened with concern. She felt almost guilty putting Johnny through this. It was enough that he'd been harassed and threatened by Skip and his friends; he didn't need abuse from the DA too. Blake didn't seem to remember that Johnny had come voluntarily—to help the prosecution's case, or perhaps to fulfill an obligation to himself. She didn't know what the boy's motives were, but she doubted he had anything personal to gain, and perhaps a lot to lose.

Blake went quiet, considering his notes. When he looked up, his eyes were locked on Johnny. "What have you got against Skip Sinclair, Johnny?" he said abruptly. "What did he do to you?"

Cat's heartbeat went staccato. She watched breathlessly as Johnny's hands coiled into fists, and the scowl on his face turned explosive. She threw out a hand to stop the boy as he stepped forward. "What are you getting at, Wheeler?" she asked, steel underscoring the lowered tone of her voice.

"The truth," Blake said, "I want the truth, that's all."

Johnny moaned out an expletive under his breath.

A flash of outrage propelled Cat toward Blake's desk. "He's telling the truth, can't you see that?" *Don't you believe anyone?* her mind cried. *You sure as hell didn't believe me ten years ago when I tried to tell you I wasn't guilty!*

"He's not on trial here!" she said, gesturing toward Johnny. "You're harassing your own witness. *"Why?"*

Cat stopped herself. She was shaking from head to toe, and unsure in her fury what she'd actually said and what she'd thought. By the look on Wheeler's face, she knew she'd crossed the line. In the next jumble of seconds she realized that she'd not only lost her objectivity, she'd personalized the situation. It was Johnny's truthfulness at issue here, not hers.

"I believe him whether you do or not," she said flatly.

"You'll vouch for the veracity of his story?"

Cat glanced at Johnny's bent and sullen posture, and for the first time since she'd met him, it occurred to her that he might be fabricating. What if he *was* out to settle some old score with Skip Sinclair? She drew in a deep breath of air and brought her head up a notch. "Of course, I'll vouch for him," she said, returning to Johnny's side.

Blake tapped out a slow, steady beat on the notepad with his pencil. "Good," he said, "I'll take that under consideration."

The anger Cat had barely quelled flared again. This man was impossible! "You do that," she said.

A tense silence ensued. Even Johnny fidgeted uneasily and looked from Cat to Blake as though he might be called upon to referee the two warring adults.

Cat crossed her arms, her index finger working like a metronome against the silk material of her blouse. Blake's pencil beat out counterpoint. The tension stretched and snapped as the office door flew open and a stunning blond woman entered. She waltzed straight for Blake's desk, seemingly oblivious of his visitors.

"Did you forget our lunch date?" she asked with a silvery laugh. "You, me, and daddy at the Plaza?" She slid onto his desk, all seductive eyelashes and smiles, and tapped her watch crystal. "You're late, sweet stuff."

Blake turned an interesting shade of crimson,

Johnny mumbled something under his breath, and Cat gaped in disbelief.

"Bad timing, Linda," Blake said, "I've got—"

"Timing, schmiming." She tweaked his tie. "You work too hard, Mr. Wheeler. You've got to loosen up!" Upon which, over Blake's protests, she proceeded to try to undo his tie altogether.

Cat watched the performance in astonished silence. *Now we know how he came by the casual look,* she thought. Of the many impulses that sparked her brain in the next seconds, the one that compelled her to action was the mushrooming belief that Blake Wheeler was totally lacking in professionalism. He'd torpedoed the meeting with her client. Beyond that, a district attorney had no business cavorting with blondes in front of impressionable teenagers. The fact that Johnny had undoubtedly seen far worse didn't dampen Cat's indignation at all. Blake Wheeler ought to be disciplined, she decided, mentally clicking off the possibilities. Disbarment? Impeachment? *Dismemberment?*

She cleared her throat. Loudly.

The marauding female released Blake's tie and glanced over her shoulder. She seemed genuinely disconcerted. "Blake! Why didn't you tell me you had visitors?"

"Don't let us interrupt," Cat said with all the icy contempt she could summon. "We were just leaving." She grabbed Johnny by the arm and hustled him toward the door.

Blake rose, straightening his tie. "Cat—"

"Catherine," she muttered.

"Get lost, Romeo," Johnny fired at Blake over his shoulder.

Cat was reaching for the doorknob when a hand closed on her shoulder. "We're not finished," Blake said.

It took Cat a moment to register that he'd actually left his desk—and the blonde—to intercept her. Somehow she hadn't imagined him caring enough to expend the effort.

"Linda's my ex-wife," he explained. "She didn't realize—"

Linda? Ex-wife? A bubble of memory burst in Cat's head. Linda Delahunt and Blake had been high school sweethearts, the prom king and queen, the couple most likely. Linda's beauty and wit was widely admired and envied, Cat notably among the latter group despite her tender years.

"I don't care who she is, Mr. Wheeler," Cat said abruptly, facing him. Her throat stung with an emotion that went far deeper than anger. "Your conduct was unprofessional and unbecoming in a public servant. You've embarrassed me, my client, *and* yourself. Don't ever let this happen again."

On that ringing note of moral indignation she took her young client in hand and left. As she and Johnny strode toward the bank of elevators on the fourth floor, Cat tasted triumph. It was sudden and fleeting, but it was sweet. The ex-jailbird had just told His Highness, the DA, where to get off!

Unfortunately, her exhilaration descended with the elevator. By the time she and Johnny reached the ground floor, she was tasting something else, a bittersweet premonition of despair. She wasn't sorry she'd upbraided Blake Wheeler. He'd had it coming. But everything she'd hoped to accomplish through the meeting may have been jeopardized—the sense of solidarity with Johnny, the mature, businesslike relationship with Wheeler. It was entirely possible that she'd blown her one opportunity to prove that she could handle herself like a professional.

The old elevator creaked and groaned, taking an inordinate amount of time to settle in at the street level. Cat pushed the DOOR OPEN button repeatedly, but the contraption wouldn't be hurried. Hazarding a glance at Johnny, she caught him studying her with open curiosity. An odd energy lit his normally sullen expression. If Cat had known the boy better, she would have recognized it as admiration, with a little awe mixed in. For the first time in a long while Johnny Drescher was impressed. Since Cat didn't know him, she put an altogether different connotation on it. She assumed he thought that she was one crazy lady. Well, maybe she was.

Johnny looked away from her and shuffled his feet. "Tough stuff," he said.

"I beg your pardon."

"You—" He grinned down at his sneakers. "You're pretty tough stuff."

Cat registered the praise with a quiet smile and a quickening pulse. High praise indeed, she realized.

As the door finally opened, Johnny came out of his slump and looked up at her, laughter gurgling in his throat. "You really fried his shorts!"

Cat almost didn't make it out of the elevator. Her eyes bugged with surprised mirth as she mouthed the words, "Excuse me?"

Johnny seemed to find that hilarious. He clapped a hand to his mouth, stifling the honking sound of his own laughter, and the sight of him was more than enough to unhinge Cat. She lost it, lost it totally. The tension and anxiety she'd been holding in burbled up in a fizzy geyser of hysteria. "I did, didn't I?" She tried to whisper and squeaked instead. "I fried his *shorts.*"

They attracted quite a crowd while making their exit from the courthouse, Johnny hee-hawing like a demented barnyard animal and Cat clutching her stomach and shushing him.

"Johnny, behave," she said, knowing full well that she was as much to blame for their lunacy as he was. By the time they reached her car, Cat finally had a grip on herself.

"They're going to arrest us for disturbing the peace," she warned, half-serious as she looked up and down the street.

"Bummer," he said, "we're both ex-cons."

The energy in Johnny's eyes riveted Cat's attention. And this time she saw it clearly for what it was. Admiration, perhaps even an offering of friendship, lurked in his hazel irises. Her shoulders rose with a sigh. How odd that the damage she'd done with Blake Wheeler may have cemented her relationship with Johnny. Life had its trade-offs.

She motioned toward her car. "Can I drop you somewhere?"

He thought about it, then shook his head. "Naw, I'd rather walk."

A question came to mind as she watched him work at his jacket zipper. She was almost afraid to ask it as silence settled in around them. "How do you feel about testifying now, Johnny?"

He considered the idea from under skeptical eyebrows, and then he grinned and faked a right cross to an imaginary opponent. "Let me at 'em."

Cat's relief left her slightly light-headed. Her sense of predestination about the meeting had been on target after all. It *had* gone exactly as it was supposed to. "Good, Johnny, good," she said, grabbing both of his hands in her enthusiasm. When he turned red and stuttery, she gave him a quick squeeze and let go. "I'll see you tomorrow then? We'll talk some more?"

He nodded and loped off down the street. Watching his awkward, coltish movements, Cat laughed and felt her heart fill with something as sad as it was happy. Who loves ya, kid? she thought, remembering the question her father whispered to her each night before she went to bed. A mist veiled her eyes. She had loved Vince D'Angelo beyond reason. He'd been the stable element in her impetuous youth, and the peacekeeper in her relationship with her mother. "You and your mom are just too much alike, Cat," he'd told her often, and somehow that simple reassurance had comforted her after a run-in with her mother.

But there was no Vince D'Angelo to smooth the way now. The mill accident had taken his life two days before Cat's thirteenth birthday. Initially the loss had seemed unendurable, almost as though some vital part of her had been amputated. It had forced her to look inside and find ways to survive. Eventually she'd discovered her own capacity for ingenuity and resourcefulness, and even though her judgment hadn't always been wise in their use, in the long run, her gut-level instincts had paid off. She was here, wasn't she? A counselor, a paid professional.

She walked around her car and opened the door, letting the memories recede. The past was painful. She tried not to think about it any more than she had to, but she needed to remember its lessons. Now, more than ever, she had to stay in touch with her hunches and play them out. Wheeler was an unpredictable man, even frightening on some deeper, personal level. Still, he could be dealt with. Anyone could once you knew what they wanted. It was a simple rule of survival she'd learned in Purdy Hall. A nervous smile flickered as she let herself into the Mustang convertible. What *did* he want? she wondered, glancing up at his window. . . .

"My, my, if you don't look like somebody just swiped your Dick Tracy decoder ring," Linda Delahunt exclaimed softly.

Blake let his ex-wife's observation pass without comment. He stood at the window of his office, his attention fixed on the mahogany-haired woman and teenager on the street below. They were giggling like a couple of kids in church, and if his hunch was right, their laughter was at his expense. Something that might have been anger collected in the muscles of Blake's jaw, except that it felt more like grudging admiration than anger. Whatever it was, the reaction brought an interesting awareness. He wasn't used to being the butt of anyone's joke.

Cat D'Angelo's back was to him and her stance drew his eyes to the attenuated line of her spine—a sloping S-curve that arced into a delicately rounded rump and straight, boyish hips. She looked slender and streamlined. And like her name, feline. Including the claws.

His body's response was a slow riptide of energy that came from somewhere deep in his solar plexus. He rode with the sensation awhile, even considered letting it play itself out—until a flicker of movement brought his attention back to Cat's interaction with Johnny.

They weren't laughing anymore. They were talking, and the teenager seemed transformed. He was animated and alive as he grinned and punched the air. Blake was curiously charmed by the camaraderie between them. And then he watched as Cat caught hold of Johnny's hands, and the boy went flame red and jerky limbed. A moment later Johnny was sprinting down the street. Another victim of Cat D'Angelo's fatal allure, Blake thought, his eyes on the fleeing boy. Temptress or not, she certainly had a way of turning the male species into bumbling idiots.

Something had to be done about her, Blake decided. In more ways than one. She was hotheaded and unpredictable, and her performance in his office had made it clear that she was going to be difficult to work with, if not impossible. Turning over several options in his mind, Blake decided none of them appealed to him at the moment. He knew he could make her life uncomfortable if he chose. At the very least he could have her replaced as Johnny's counselor. But none of those things would solve his immediate problem.

He wanted her all to himself for as long as it took to solve the enigma of Catherine D'Angelo. The mystery in her smoky eyes, in her sultry, angry red lips was obsessing his mind. It was her contradictions that mystified him, and the force of will that contained them all in one woman. It was her erotic darkness, her hidden sadness . . .

"I know that look, Mr. Wheeler," Linda said. "It means you're formulating a plan of attack."

The words registered on Blake's nervous system first, more as sounds than meaning. It took him a moment to bring them into focus. He had forgotten his ex-wife was in the office.

He turned to the beautiful blonde who was decorating his office chair and met her knowing smile. Linda Delahunt did know him. She still referred to their eighteen-month marriage as a crash course in the care and feeding of Blake Wheeler. To her credit, she'd almost immediately seen that she wasn't suited for a life in the shadow of another prominent politician.

"I won't go through that again for any man," she'd told Blake when she asked him for a divorce. "My formative years were spent as a walking, talking campaign poster—hizzoner's daughter." The dissolution of their marriage had been mercifully quick and free of acrimony. It had saved their friendship.

Blake sucked in his cheeks, effecting a gaunt look. "Did it ever occur to you that this 'look' means I haven't eaten since breakfast?"

She studied him over elegant, peach-tinted cheekbones. "Tell me about the woman, Blake. Who is she?"

"Woman?"

"Oh, please—don't play innocent with me. She had you going, didn't she, Wheeler? That dark-eyed hellcat. I don't think I've ever seen you so flustered." Linda came out of the chair and swung her blond pageboy into place. "And by the way, if looks could kill, I'd be on life support right now."

Blake made no attempt to hide his confusion. "What do you mean?"

"She didn't like me, Blake, not one bit. She didn't want me anywhere near you. I could see it in her eyes."

Blake gave Linda a look that questioned her sanity. "If you're suggesting that her interest in me is anything other than hostile, you're dreaming."

Linda shook her head. "A woman knows about these things, Blake. That lady has some definite notions in her head where you're concerned. Whether they involve passion or murder, I couldn't say, but I'd bet on the first."

"Right, she's passionate about murdering me."

Linda wagged a finger at him. "Lord," she said, checking her watch, "Daddy's going to murder both of us! Let's go."

She was halfway to the door before she realized Blake wasn't following her.

"I can't," he said, fending off her displeasure with a nod toward the stacks of paper on his desk. "I've got some pressing things to do."

Her answer was a quick, sexy smile. "Sure you do. And I want you to know that I understand . . . but Daddy won't."

Blake turned back to the window as Linda left. He was just in time to see Cat slide into the driver's seat of the Mustang and look up at his window. Sunlight ignited her dark eyes and sprinkled ruby fire in her mahogany hair. She met his gaze for a moment—long enough to alter his heartbeat—but for some odd reason all he could see were her lips . . . red and wet and shiny.

And then he remembered.

Years ago in his office she'd worn that same lipstick—cherry red, glistening. And her fingernails. Slick as water, red as cherries too. He hadn't known what to make of Cat D'Angelo back then. She was terra incognita for a twenty-five-year-old deputy DA fresh out of Stanford Law and looking to set the world on fire. He remembered thinking that the lipstick made her mouth look shiny and ripe, like fruit. He also remembered thinking she was too young for lipstick like that, lipstick that made a man think of fruit . . .

By the time Blake returned to the present, the

Mustang convertible was gone. Lunch-hour traffic poured by in an even stream, and courthouse workers gathered on the steps gossiping and digging into their brown bag lunches. But Blake didn't see any of it. He wasn't looking. He was staring at the spot where the Mustang had been. He was thinking about the woman with the lush red mouth. And about the fact that she wasn't too young anymore.

The lightninglike energy flashed low and deep, connecting neural pathways that were elemental and quick to arouse. He wasn't a man who acted on impulse. He valued control too much. And intellect. But it was impulse, pure and simple, that was fueling him now. *He wanted her. Alone. All to himself.*

Warnings flashed in his mind. She'd been hurt before. It was written all over her: FRAGILE, HANDLE WITH CARE. Don't complicate her life, Wheeler, he told himself. Or yours. But none of the caveats had a chance against the voltage building up inside him.

Something had to be done about Cat D'Angelo. *Soon.*

Five

Cat had good news and bad news to report at the center's staff meeting that afternoon. Four of the agency's five full-time counselors were present in the small conference room, including herself and Gwen. Everyone listened with great interest to her announcement about Johnny's change of heart. She even got a round of applause when she told them he was going to testify. Her client's *enfant-terrible* reputation was well established at the center, it seemed.

"Blake must be pleased," Gwen said.

Cat tipped her hand back and forth in a not-exactly gesture. That was the bad news. "There was a difference of opinion," she said, "and then our meeting was cut short."

"Difference of opinion?"

Cat's explanation was interrupted by two loud raps on the conference room door. Gwen had barely got out a response before the door swung open and Blake Wheeler filled the threshold.

He glanced around the office and fastened his steel-gray eyes on Cat as he addressed her supervisor. "Can I borrow one of your counselors, Gwen?"

Cat rose from her chair. "What for?"

"For about an hour," Blake said, nailing her to the floor with a dark look. "I want to discuss what happened this morning."

"I'm in a meeting."

"Cat," Gwen said, standing, "I think you should step outside and discuss this with Mr. Wheeler."

Gwen's tone brooked no argument. Cat glanced at her watch, aware of the expectant stares of her fellow counselors. With a tight sigh she pushed out of her chair, rounded the table, and swept past Blake Wheeler. What other choice did she have?

As the conference door slammed shut behind her, she prepared herself to deal firmly but courteously with him. She could not talk now, she would tell him, but perhaps they could arrange something for later in the week.

She turned, and the words froze in her throat. He was angry—or something very close to it. Cat had only seen that look in his eyes one other time. She hadn't had the experience to know what it meant then. Or what he wanted. Now she knew. Desire, hunger, physical need, she couldn't put a name on it, but she knew exactly what it meant, that silver heat in his eyes.

"Let's go," he said. "My car's outside."

She didn't have time to ask him where. He had her by the arm and out the door before she could get her bearings.

Stunned by his forcefulness and the prodigious length of his stride, she found herself concentrating on how to keep up with him rather than the objections pinging around in her head.

It wasn't until they were in Blake's Corvette and speeding away from the center that Cat recovered sufficiently to ask where they were going. He didn't respond immediately, and when he did answer, she couldn't hear him. His voice was lost in the violent perturbations of the Corvette's chassis as he accelerated over the jutting Southern Pacific tracks.

The engine roared in protest as he geared the car into low, hung a right turn, and took a side road that led out of town. Watching him effortlessly manipulate the powerful machine, Cat was unwillingly drawn by the way he'd pushed the sleeves of his sweater up over his elbows. He might be playing the "just folks" image for all it was worth, she admitted, but he did have good forearms—tanned and muscular, generously swept with golden hair.

She was equally struck by the controlling force of his grip on the stick shift. He was a large-boned man, with an enormous span to his palm and the seemingly telepathic grip of an athlete. His fingers worked and stroked the meshwork like a delicate musical instrument, and all Cat could think about as she watched was how he'd taken control of her so many years ago with that same grace of precision and masculine force. He had gripped her slender wrist in his huge hand, and without hurting her, he'd shocked her into realizing what she was doing. "You've got the wrong guy," he'd said quietly. "I don't bargain that way."

Cat's heart went crazy as she allowed herself to remember the entire incident from its beginning— the anger, the power plays, the way he'd tried to convince her to testify against Cheryl. "I don't rat on friends," she had told him defiantly.

"Even if it means your freedom?" He had risen from his chair and sat on the edge of his desk in front of her chair. "If you don't testify against her, you'll go to jail *with* her, Cat."

Jail? Fear crept into her muscles, paralyzing her. Even the childish outrage that burned in Cat's heart had failed her in that moment. She'd almost given in, promised him whatever he wanted, until she'd seen the flicker of triumph in his eyes. That was when she realized he was manipulating her, playing on her deepest fears in order to pit her against her friend. A sense of betrayal had stung through her, and then she'd been furious at herself for imagining that he might know—or care—enough about her to think in those terms. He was only doing his job, "leaning" on a potential witness. That was when she'd decided that two could play Blake Wheeler's game. . . .

"Do you like my sweater?" she'd asked, touching the neckline the way she'd seen Cheryl do when her friend talked to men. Cheryl was beautiful and smart about all sorts of things that Cat barely understood. Cheryl was everything Cat wasn't.

"Do you think I'm pretty?" Her voice had wavered as she'd asked.

"Yes . . . you're very pretty."

The way he let his eyes drift over her and then stopped himself told Cat he meant it. Perhaps it was that glint of interest that gave her the impetus to go on. She'd been dreaming about Blake Wheeler since the tender age of thirteen, ever since the unforgettable day he'd shown up at their house shortly after her father's death. The infatuation was compelling, and yet for years after the incident in Blake's office, Cat was to wonder how she'd actually found the courage to approach him. It must have been an instinct for survival that overrode everything else . . . fear, propriety, *everything.*

Whatever it was that freed Cat at that moment, she acted on it. She conquered her paralyzing fears long enough to walk over to him and boldly meet his eyes. And then she startled a gasp out of him as crimson fingernails glided over his trousered thigh. "Maybe there's something you want even more than you want my testimony?" she said.

His jaw locked and she could feel the muscles of his leg tightening beneath her fingers. Her pulse skyrocketed with the crazy terror that panic brings, but she forced herself to continue what she was doing, stroking softly.

"You don't want to do this," he warned her.

"Yes, I do . . . don't you?"

She leaned toward him then, shaking with fear and adrenaline, intending to kiss him, but instead, she heard the low, angry hiss of his breath.

He caught hold of her wrist and locked her in place with a force that was unexpected and disorienting. There was power and anger in his features;

there was disbelief. His eyes questioned her sanity. "You're some kind of wild child, aren't you?"

Cat's heart nearly strangled her. Desperate, she tossed her head, and mahogany hair tumbled wildly around her face.

"Is that . . . what you want?" she asked. "A wild child?" That was when she'd seen it, the lightning flash of desire in his eyes that told her she was right about him. That *was* what he wanted. She moved against him and gasped as he used his strength to hold her back.

With ferocious control and stunning precision, he forced her to her knees and said, "You've got the wrong guy. I don't bargain that way."

His eyes pierced her like a blade. No one had ever looked at her that way before, as though she was something wanton and seductive, a harlot or a witch.

Shame had flooded her then, nearly annihilated her. . . .

Cat wrenched herself back to the present with a force of will that left her shaken and sickeningly dizzy. Heat burned the back of her neck and her heart slammed in her chest.

The present brought no relief, only a more immediate threat. She was trapped in the car with him. That realization became more acute with every ticking second. The air was thick with his presence, from the piquant citrus of his after-shave to the expensive leather of his shoes. Cat wanted out of the car. If he touched her, even accidentally, she would scream. She would go crazy out of her mind.

She clenched a hand against her stomach and held it there as though she might explode like a sprung grenade if she removed it. All she could do was sit still, perfectly still, and pray for self-control.

The low roar of the engine penetrated her rigidity. She felt its reverberations at the base of her spine and in the soles of her feet. It was warm and lifelike and oddly threatening to a body in which even the blood seemed to have stopped flowing. She was aware of Blake next to her, glancing at her—once, twice—watching her curiously. *Don't let him ask me what's wrong,* she thought.

He geared the car down, and the engine roared in protest.

They turned onto a gravel road marked PRIVATE, and Cat realized where they were going. He was taking her to his parents' cabin on the bay. The Wheeler family compound in bygone days, she remembered, and suddenly her head was swimming with data. There'd been a reconciliation between Blake and his parents some years ago, if she recalled correctly from Gwen's letters. More recently the elder Wheelers had retired and moved to Florida. Apparently Blake was now handling the property.

Cat felt as though her mind was idling too high in a stalled-out body. As they pulled into the driveway she took in details with the thoroughness and detachment of a property assessor. The cabin was a huge, rambling affair with gleaming bay windows and wooden decks all around. The landscaped grounds sloped to a white boat dock that snaked over placid, slate-blue water. So this was how the other half lived on the weekends, she thought, her hand still clutched to her stomach. The house dominated her field of vision. If it was a "cabin," her family home across the tracks was a lean-to shack.

Blake cut the car's engine. "We'll be able to talk here without interruptions," he said.

Unreasoning panic gripped Cat. For an instant she was the child again, on her knees, and paralyzed by the sexual static in a powerful man's eyes.

"All right," she said, fumbling the car door open. She let herself out and without waiting for him, began to walk toward the lake. Loose rocks cut through the thin soles of her pumps, and a brisk breeze off the bay whipped tendrils of hair into her eyes. When she reached the dock, she walked clear to its end without stopping.

The moorage moaned and groaned under her feet,

murmuring to her like ancient soothsayers of foolish beginnings and dark endings. She felt the warnings with her senses more than her mind, and
gooseflesh shivered on her arms. The dock swayed,
and she was just learning its rhythms as it began to
roll against her movements.

He was coming. Cat fought to keep her balance as
the moorage rocked violently. Emotions tangled up
inside her, past and present inextricably snarled.
For all these years she had avoided exploring her
feelings for him beyond the anger. The anger was
safe. Now she needed desperately to find another
shield to throw up. What had he wanted? To talk?
No, that was to be avoided at all costs. Talk about
what? And then she remembered. Johnny.

The soothsayers whispered again, and then the
dock went still and silent.

"Is something wrong?"

It was Blake, behind her. He was close, concerned.
She could hear the weight of it in his voice.

Ten years ago she would have been grateful for
any show of kindness from him, any hint of sensitivity. But not now. Kindness could wreck her now.
She was too exposed, too needy. Remembering had
reopened all her wounds.

"You're cold," he said. "Do you want my jacket?"

She shook her head.

"What is it then?"

At her silence he persisted. "Hey, it can't be that
bad." His voice took on a huskiness that was almost
gentle. "Is there some problem? Maybe I can help."

She closed her eyes and shook her head again.
Why is he doing this to me? she thought, her throat
tightening. *Why is he suddenly pretending to care—*

She stiffened as his hand grazed her shoulder. If he
touched her, she would scream. She would go crazy.

"Cat, you're shaking. Tell me what's wrong."

A board creaked beneath her, and the sound was
urgent, a child's cry of bewilderment. You hurt me,
she thought, that's what's wrong. Not my body. You

never left a mark on me physically. But emotionally, you nearly destroyed me. You stripped away my pride and what was left of my dignity. How could you do that to a terrified young girl? How could you do that to someone as desperate and lost as I was?

He touched her arm and she flinched.

"Why did you do that to Johnny?" She whirled on him, her eyes damning him with accusations.

"Do? I questioned him. That's my job."

"You alienated him."

"No, I made contact."

His golden hair flashed in the sunlight, and a strange transfiguration took place in Cat's mind. Haloed by the bay's fiery brilliance, he looked preternatural, like a god, incapable of human failing, invulnerable to human suffering. The vision was there and gone in an instant, but she had seen it before— the same man, the same burst of sunlight—just days after her father's death.

She shook off the image. Blake Wheeler wasn't a god. He was mortal, and he carried the same burdens of the flesh that she did. "You accused him of having something against Skip Sinclair," she said. "You implied that he was lying."

The mooring rolled with some deep, unseen current. Cat stumbled back and moaned softly as he reached out and caught her hand. Or was it the dock that had moaned? The sudden heat, the strength of him, penetrated through to her delicate bones. He had too much power, this man, too much control over others, even in the sheltering warmth of his hand. She pulled free of him and felt a clutch of sensation in her stomach. "Why did you do it?"

The pupils in his eyes narrowed fractionally, then he looked beyond her to the water. "Johnny has a bad reputation," he said at last. "The defense will go after him with everything they've got. They'll destroy him if they can. I had to find out if he's a reliable witness. If he cracks under cross-examination, he's no good to me."

All she truly comprehended were the last four words—*no good to me.* The implications appalled her. "Is winning the case all that matters to you? My God, don't you care about anything? Don't people matter at all?"

The anger and hurt in her voice lashed out at Blake like a whip. It crackled along his nerve endings. He remembered physical beatings from his father that had carried less censure. Her assault was aimed at his character rather than at his body, but it stung like hell nevertheless.

The need to defend himself was compelling. "I prosecute killers, rapists, thieves," he told her. "I keep the streets clean for people like you."

"You also prosecute people like me."

Blake had no answer for that. He was guilty as charged. He had done what the law required in her case, but she seemed to be saying that he had sacrificed her in the process. He wanted to deny it, but he couldn't. Maybe because it was true. Or maybe because something crazy was happening inside him. Something that had never happened before. He wasn't breathing as far as he could tell. His heart wasn't even beating. Beyond that, he couldn't take his eyes off Cat D'Angelo.

Her face was flushed with anger, and she was aiming her chin at him like a weapon. But none of those signals registered because the message hidden in her eyes was completely paradoxical. It was a flash of pain that cut to the quick. It defined her. It obliterated all the contradictions and told him who she was—a soul-bandaged child. The soft glimmering of agony in her dark eyes made his chest squeeze like a fist.

Blake's heart surged. He forgot what she was accusing him of, forgot everything but the signal she was telegraphing. For several seconds it evoked emotions that were completely alien to him: helplessness, confusion, and guilt. And then it made him want her more. Suddenly he understood his obsession with Cat D'Angelo. *He had to make the pain in her eyes go away because he had put it there.*

He knew now what she was telling him and what she had been trying to tell him all along. He had wounded her in his zeal for justice or glory or whatever it was he'd been after then. She'd been a casualty of the system, *his* casualty.

The insight brought him back. "I care . . ." he said.

Cat shook her head wildly and turned away from him. Her need to deny him was as strong as his need had been to deny her accusations. He didn't care. Blake Wheeler was genetically incapable of caring. She'd heard the unsteadiness in his voice. He sounded almost defeated, and that possibility confounded her. She wouldn't have believed him capable of an admission of surrender. He wasn't. She clung to that belief. He wasn't.

"I'll talk to Johnny," he said. "If there's been any damage, I'll repair it."

Cat pressed a hand to her throat and felt her pulse trip painfully beneath her fingers. Repair the damage? Did he know what he was doing? Did he know what that kind of a promise meant to her?

"Turn around, Cat," he said. "Look at me."

"Why . . . ?"

"Your eyes . . . the sadness."

She froze when he touched her, froze at the outrageous suggestion in his words and the intimacy in his hands. "There is no sadness in my eyes," she said. "Don't do this to me."

"What? What am I doing to you?"

He knew. He had to know that he was tearing down the only barrier she had left. He was making her forget that she hated him at a time when she needed desperately to preserve that excoriating emotion, to keep on hating him.

"Cat . . ."

Her nerves were oversensitized, exposed. She could even feel the air on her skin. His voice was roughened with emotion and so irresistibly grainy, she imagined it floating over her, riffling the fine hair on her arms. A quiver of sensation stirred inside her, low and alarming.

"You're not doing anything to me—" She shook her head abruptly. "Not *that*, anyway."

Blake watched a shudder pass through her body, and he had to fight the urge to take her in his arms. He was doing things to her. God, yes, he was doing things to her. Her body gave up the quick, sweet heat of a woman in conflict. Her voice had altered when she'd spoken, and the shake in her breathing had sent a live current of electricity through him. She wasn't invulnerable. She was terrified of every touch, every word. Underneath all her stunning ferocity there were needs she wanted desperately to protect.

The realization made Blake gentle. It made him hard.

He caught his breath as the swelling in his groin sensitized him to every shimmer of movement, even her breathing. Her shoulders rose faintly, swiftly. And there was a slash of crimson mottling the creamy skin of her neck. She was so beautiful, so profoundly threatened, she made him ache.

Of all the impulses firing in Blake's brain, the one that promised to override every other consideration was the drive for contact. Deep contact. He wanted to take her in his arms and burn away the sadness. It was a physical need beyond anything he'd experienced. Its force astonished him. Touch her, man, take her, his body raged. Lay her down on this swaying dock and fill her beautiful body with yours. Rock her until she comes apart, then put her back together, man, tenderly, *tenderly.*

The drive to be with her tested his years of self-denial. It tested his will. He had learned control at the knee of a self-made man, his empire-building father, and those lessons, however brutal, had been effective. Now they allowed him to pull back, to remember what was at stake.

She was explosive—a beautiful, desperate time bomb. If he handled her carelessly, she could annihilate them both. Defusing her anger would be as delicate a task as a bomb squad's, but if he could do it— His mind tightened, sharpened. If he could do it, the tears would come and she would open herself to him, her heart, her body. God, he wanted that. He couldn't remember wanting anything more.

Cat gripped her arms against a sudden gust of wind. She had no more awareness of Blake's needs than a stalked animal knows that danger is imminent. She only knew that he wanted something. Men like him always wanted something.

"I have to go," she said, her voice tight. "Let me go."

"I'm not stopping you."

She turned and her shoulder brushed his chest. The accidental contact was startling. She caught her breath and arched her neck automatically, thinking he was going to touch her, or take her into his arms. Anticipation rippled her nerves, and her imagination spun out a scenario of being swept up in his embrace, kissed and caressed until she couldn't breathe.

But he didn't touch her. Nor did he move out of her way.

"What do you want?" she asked.

Blake almost laughed. She wouldn't believe it if he told her. He didn't believe it! He wanted love, he wanted life, he wanted hard, sweet sex with her. What do you think of that, Ms. Time Bomb? What do you think of that?

"I want to talk about us," he said.

"Us?"

Blake could have predicted the stab of panic in her eyes, but he couldn't have predicted what was happening inside Cat. As she met his gaze, she felt herself dropping, a wind-rider caught in a powerful downdraft. The plummeting sensation in her stomach was sudden and sharp. The dock seemed to go out from under her feet, and as she imagined herself falling, she caught a glimpse of something in her mind that riveted her.

Surrender.

Even the glimpse of such naked emotion was terrifying to Cat. It entranced and enthralled her. It was the source of her panic. It was the wellspring of her deepest need. To be touched, to be loved. She shuddered in silence and raised her face to his.

By the time he did touch her, the shuddering was deep inside her. It was emotional and sexual and beautiful. No, she thought, this is impossible. This isn't happening. *Not with this man. Not with him . . .*

He curved his hand to her throat and drew her to him.

"What do I do, Cat?" he asked. "How do I make the sadness go away?"

The question rocked her softly, reverberating in the echo chamber her senses had become. *Not this man. Not him. He's hurt you too much . . .*

"Sweet, sad, Cat." He caressed the underside of her chin with long, long strokes of his thumb. The sensations were soft and erotic and thrilling, and they accomplished exactly what they were supposed to, Cat realized, bringing her head up sharply. He wanted her to look up at him. He wanted her throat arched, her head tilted back.

No, Cat! He's hurt you too much.

"Don't," she whispered. "Not you . . ."

"Yes, Cat, me," he said. "It has to be me."

He bent toward her, and his lips touched hers with a lightning stroke of tenderness. Cat swallowed the moan in her throat. In all her guilty dreams of kissing Blake Wheeler—and there had been many—she had never imagined it as tender. She had never imagined a sweetness so sharp that it would fill her throat and tear through her heart like a poignant memory. Was this how lovers kissed? Lovers who had hurt each other and now needed to be very, very cautious? Lovers whose wounds weren't healed?

Age-old warnings stirred inside her. She should have resisted, she wanted to resist, but as his lips brushed over hers she felt yearnings flare up inside her—a wrenchingly sweet need to deepen the kiss, to be held and crushed in his arms. She had imagined him as self-absorbed, an egotistical lover who would take what he wanted and assume that being with him was enough for any woman. A night with Blake Wheeler. A night in heaven! She had imagined herself rejecting him, ordering him out of her bed and out of her life. She had imagined all of those things so many times . . . but never *tenderness*.

His mouth was warm. It was as vibrant as the water sparkling around them. She touched his arm, perhaps to push him away, and then his lips drifted over hers, and her touch became a caress. Her fingers shimmered over heat and muscle, and she felt a sudden, sharp need to be closer.

All of her attention was focused on the extraordinary thing that was happening to her. A kiss, she told herself, *it was just a kiss.* But he touched her with such rare tenderness. His fingers plucked at her nerve-strings as if she were a delicate musical instrument. His mouth transfused her with fire and drained her of energy at the same time. And when at last his arms came around her and brought her up against him, she felt a sweet burst of physical longing that saturated her senses.

She had dreamt of his body, too. And the feel of him now was almost more reality than she could stand. His thighs were steel, and his pelvic bones dug into her flesh. He was hard, righteously hard, and even the slightest shifts in pressure put her in touch with her own keening emptiness.

His tongue stroked her lips, and she opened them to him slowly, irresistibly. On some level she knew she was playing a sword dance with her own emotions, tempting fate, tempting heartbreak, but the sensations were so exquisite, she couldn't stop herself. They seemed as inevitable and sensual as the deep currents swaying beneath them.

The first gliding touch of his tongue against hers electrified her. A gasp welled in her throat as he grazed her teeth and tingled sensitive surfaces. The penetration was deliciously languid and deep. By the time he lifted his mouth from hers, she was shocked and reeling from the taste of him.

The urge to push him away was instinctive.

"No, Cat," he said softly, inexplicably, "it's mine now. The sadness inside you is mine."

Studying her face, searching her eyes for something, he smoothed her hair and murmured melting suggestions that she couldn't consciously decipher. They tugged at her sweetly, hotly, pulling her insides to and fro, eliciting yearnings. Cat's first awareness of them was a kind of vague astonishment. It was deep and thrilling, what was happening inside her, like eddying water, like the sucking and pulling of currents. She'd never known such oddly captivating sensations.

The wooden dock creaked and the bay swelled gently beneath them, tugging at the pilings. Cat sighed as the rhythms of the sea and the man worked their enchantment. His hands *were* telepathic. They sought out all her tender spots. His fingers moved in concert with the deep currents, stroking the sideswells of her breasts, arousing her nerves to rivulets of excitement.

"Wild," he murmured as he cupped her breasts in his palms. "Wild, wild child."

Cat's stomach tightened at the words.

Dark water flashed brilliantly behind him. The moorings creaked plaintively. *Not him, child, not this man . . .*

He began to open the buttons of her blouse.

No, Cat! He's hurt you too much.

Warm, urgent hands skimmed over her skin, and Cat felt the collision of opposing forces. With fascinated detachment she watched the first button of her blouse come free and realized that Blake Wheeler was about to take from her one of the few really precious things she had left to give—physical love. The thought catapulted her back to reality. It horrified her.

His fingers brushed the cleft of her breasts and the raw sensuality of it took her breath away.

"No!" She clutched her blouse together and stepped back from him.

"What is it?"

She shook her head, forcing out the words. "This is wrong."

"Wrong? What do you mean?" He searched her features, his voice compelling. "No . . . this was supposed to happen. Neither one of us could have stopped it."

"I'm stopping it. I'm stopping it now!" She pushed past him and strode toward the end of the dock.

"Where are you going?" he called after her. "Cat! You can't walk."

"I have no intention of walking! Carson's market is down the street. I'll call a taxi from there."

He breathed a word that made her nerves jump. Even from her distance she heard it. Cat didn't turn back to see what he looked like, standing there on the dock, watching her storm out of his life. She didn't have to. She could vividly imagine his eyes darkening, the silver flecks turning to black.

Her heart was still racing as she reached the driveway that would take her off his property. Strands of flyaway hair clung damply to her cheek. As she brushed them away, a realization shocked her.

If this *was* her secret dream—rejecting him, scorning him the way he'd scorned her—then why did it feel like a nightmare?

Six

"Let me out— Here!"

The taxi screeched to a halt, and the driver—a grizzled veteran of many a crazy fare by the pained look on his face—turned to squint at Cat. "Sure, lady. You want out in the middle of nowhere, that's your prerogative."

She paid him, probably too much, and got out in the middle of nowhere.

The taxi rumbled away over the railroad tracks and Cat followed the tread of his tires to the first rail. There she stepped inside the dusty silver tracks and began to walk off her turmoil.

She'd done the same thing as a child. Walking the tracks had been her escape from the difficulties at home. There'd been something soothing about the endless silver ribbons, something fluid and mysterious about the places they'd come from, and where they might be going. She had imagined following the tracks as Dorothy had the Yellow Brick Road, to somewhere magical.

Unfortunately, today the old magic wasn't working.

The tracks weren't soothing enough to stop her from kicking savagely at the protruding rocks she stumbled over. Or from demanding answers of herself.

Nerves jolted up her spine as she glanced down at

her blouse and saw that she hadn't buttoned it up. *Swell,* she thought, fumbling the buttons back in place. The taxi driver must have thought he'd picked up a bimbo lunatic. She wanted to laugh, but the sound that escaped was a tight, shaking sigh. Frustration peaked inside her, fisting into a soft knot of anguish. She *was* a lunatic. Sane women didn't make out on boat docks with men they had every reason to loathe!

She had no acceptable explanation for her behavior at the moment except to put it back on Blake. He wasn't a man, or a god. He was some kind of demon. He seemed to be able to reach past her anger and touch into tender feelings she couldn't protect. He drew up longings and needs. Womanly needs. Physical longings. Even childlike yearnings for love and acceptance.

Resentment pierced her. It filled her mouth with a sharp, metallic taste, as though she'd bitten down on a copper penny. The urge to thrash around in her own negativity was nearly irresistible. Anger was safe, it was cathartic, but she couldn't indulge herself now. There were bigger questions. There was a man on the planet who seemed to have the power to override her will, and that, alone, was inconceivable to her. Cat D'Angelo's will was no puny thing. She knew, she lived with it. How had he tamed the snarling beast when she could barely keep the cage door shut?

His tenderness confounded her too. Why had he made the references to her sadness? Why the offers of help? What in the world did he want from her? The mere thought that it might be the sick triumph of seducing one of his victims made her queasy. Even Blake Wheeler wasn't that depraved. It would make more sense if she could believe that he was afraid of losing Johnny Drescher as a witness. But that didn't compute either. He'd hardly seemed that gung ho about winning the Skip Sinclair case. Truth be told, she'd had her doubts about whose side he was on.

Her rapid steps were accentuated by the silence of the forest. The sylvan beauty of her surroundings went unnoticed as she pressed forward on her journey back to town. Gravel crunched beneath her shoes, and a gray squirrel darted from out of nowhere, skittering across the tracks. What you don't see when you haven't got a gun, Cat thought bitterly—and was appalled at herself. She loved animals! It was him she wanted to gun down.

She sent another spray of pebbles flying over the rails. It was almost ludicrous that she'd once contemplated evening the score with Blake Wheeler. He'd be having a good laugh about that now if he knew. Necking on his boat dock?! Excellent strategy. Go get him, D'Angelo! Lord knew what she might have done if she'd liked the guy.

A smooth rock the size of a tennis ball lay in Cat's path. She kicked at it and connected with a solid thud.

"Ahhhh!" Her cry of pain rocketed through the deep gully that bordered the tracks. Dropping into a crouch, she clutched her foot and let out a string of expletives blue enough to melt the railroad tracks to tinfoil.

Tears blurred her vision as she sank to the ground, yanked off her shoe, and began to massage her throbbing foot. The pain was excruciating. Reverberations screamed in every nerve ending.

As her vision cleared, she saw that it wasn't a rock she'd kicked. It was a steel railroad spike! Her big toe was obviously broken. It was turning maroon before her eyes. She clenched her jaw, tears welling. "Dammit, Wheeler!" she cried. "Look what you made me do!"

Shrill and petulant, her words rang down the gully like caroling bells. Massaging doggedly, Cat winced with every echo of her voice. Forced to listen to herself damning Wheeler ad infinitum, she realized how childish she sounded.

Tears sprang to her eyes as she thought about the errors in judgment she'd made and the grief her trip-wire temper had brought her throughout her life. At sixteen, she could have been excused for some of the craziness, hormones and mothers being what they were. But even then she might have saved herself a lot of needless thrashing around if she had acknowledged her share of the responsibility for the events that led into the trial.

Much as she might want to blame Blake for everything, including the famine in Africa, it was a perfectly absurd thing to do. At least in this case. Blake Wheeler hadn't broken her toe. She had.

Gradually, as the pain eased, she began to come to uneasy terms with whom she was really angry at. For the toe. Perhaps for all of it. Yours truly, she thought, grimacing. She'd spotted the enemy, and her name was Cat D'Angelo.

The trip back to town went badly. Cat couldn't get her foot back in her pump, and she knew very little about aerobic limping. She finally removed both shoes and set out to blaze her own path through the wild grass that blanketed the shoulder of the gully.

Her family home came into view as she rounded the last in a series of curves the track took. Forlorn and deserted, the clapboard house looked ready for the wrecking ball. Still, the sight of it took her by storm. A heaviness descended on her, and her breath got trapped deep in her lungs. She hadn't realized she was so close to the old neighborhood. She nodded at the sagging front porch quickly, as though acknowledging an adversary, then she kept on walking with every intention of passing the place by.

A guilty glance over her shoulder brought her to a stop. Such a small, shabby place, she thought, saddening. And so empty now, with both of them gone.

As Cat stared at the front door, her mother's spotless housecleaning and unreachable standards came to mind. Her father's forbearance. Their arguments over how to handle their impetuous daughter rang in Cat's head. "She's contrary and too willful for her own good," her mother had insisted whenever Vince D'Angelo tried to defend his young daughter as high-spirited.

Cat had been all of those things: high-spirited, contrary, *and* willful. She had complicated her parents' lives immeasurably with her boundless curiosity and her misadventures. She'd skipped school regularly. She'd even stowed away on a bus to Portland once. Her mother had whipped her for that escapade and restricted her to the house for a month. Cat was always apologetic, always intending to make amends, but she never did change her impetuous ways. She couldn't. Life called to her, seductive and exciting. Life was good . . . until the tragedy struck.

As she turned to face the house, she was hit forcefully by the impact of that tragedy. The world had gone dark when her father was killed. She closed her eyes a moment, remembering, and even as she opened them, another memory visited her, the strange event that took place shortly after her thirteenth birthday.

Her father hadn't been gone two weeks when a man showed up at their place. Cat didn't recognize him when her mother opened the door. Sunlight poured into the room, shadowing his face and igniting his hair to liquid gold. Cat watched the man hand her mother a check, then she saw her mother shake and bend and cry. She'd never seen her mother cry before, even at the funeral.

The man embraced her mother quickly, gently, and that's when Cat had seen his face. The Wheeler boy. Lord, but he'd had such a strong, handsome face at twenty-two, sharp-boned and clean, lit with goodness, shaded with sincerity. For some reason that Cat didn't understand, tears had filled her eyes. "A miracle," she'd heard her mother whisper to him, "you're a miracle sent by God."

Blake Wheeler had let some light into Cat's life that day. In addition to offering them hope in the very tangible form of money, he was demonstrating that someone actually cared. Cat realized now that she'd taken the image of his handsome face into some secret part of her and held it there. Perhaps she'd even fallen a little bit in love.

Turning away from the house, she started down the tracks again, laden with memories so bittersweet she wished she could erase them from her past. She'd been desperately needy at that tender age, lost without her doting father. Blake's courage, his stand against his own parents and the negligence of the company they owned, his larger-than-life presence, would have turned any young girl's head. Still, it embarrassed her now to admit that she'd been hopelessly infatuated with a man who probably didn't know she existed.

Three years later in a packed courtroom there was no question about who Cat D'Angelo was. Or that Blake Wheeler knew of her existence. She was the town's bad girl. And he was its golden boy. Sworn to bring criminals to justice, even frightened sixteen-year-old girls who were half in love with him.

Cat lifted her head, steeling herself against the emotion building inside. Tears misted her eyes, the angry, accusatory tears of her childhood. He had torn her heart out in that courtroom. If he knew she was Vince D'Angelo's daughter, he'd never mentioned it, not once during the entire ordeal. Savaged pride had kept her from throwing herself on his mercy. That, and his ultimatum that she testify against her friend or be prosecuted, had convinced her that Blake Wheeler was a bastard who played at being a hero when it suited him. In her adolescent outrage she had prayed that someday he would hurt the way she hurt. And then she vowed to wipe his name from her memory.

By the time Cat reached the street the center was on, she'd begun to appreciate the wisdom of adolescent outrage. It had been an honest response to a painful situation. At least she'd known what she felt and exactly where she stood. Now she was waffling all over the place, hating him, kissing him, needing him. "Oh, *Lord.*"

Those were the words on her lips as she swung the center door open and saw Johnny Drescher slumped in one of the reception-area chairs, his hands fisted in his jeans pockets.

Shoes in hand, Cat overshot the threshold slightly and pitched into the room. "Is something wrong?"

He looked up at her and shrugged. "Not with me. You look pretty bummed, though."

She nodded at her throbbing foot and winced. "Broken toe. Kicked the football too hard, I guess."

He was trying to be cool, Cat knew, but his smile was big and goofy and heart-catching as he took in her condition. "Your football days are over."

She nodded. "Fix me an ice bag?"

He heaved himself from the chair and shuffled off toward the kitchen. Cat smiled at his departing back. "You're a prince," she called after him.

Moments later as they sat in her office, Johnny tilted back in his chair, Cat with her foot elevated, she came to a realization. Continuing to counsel Johnny meant dealing with Blake Wheeler. There would be more meetings, more tension and power-playing between the attorneys and their clients, the inevitable recriminations—and finally, a pretrial hearing.

She'd been through it before—and that was reason enough to back out now. If she had any sense left at all, she'd find someone else to handle Johnny's case.

"How's the toe?" he asked. "We could always amputate."

"Thanks, but I've grown attached to it." Returning his crooked grin, Cat considered the pathetically thin, disheveled teenager across from her and suddenly backing out seemed inconceivable. He needed an ally. *He needed her.*

Okay, she thought, conviction stirring, I can deal with Blake Wheeler if I have to. I can deal with anyone for this kid.

"Juju gums? A mint patty? How about some cheese curls?" The drugstore clerk, a skinny, ponytailed teenager, snapped her gum and made a wrinkly triangle of her nose. "What'll it be, huh?"

Blake Wheeler shook his head. He had a craving for something decadent and loaded with food additives, only he couldn't make up his mind what he wanted. The girl's gum popped like a cherry bomb. "Okay, give me the cheese curls," he said.

She obliged with a decided lack of enthusiasm.

Out on the street Blake opened the bag and was flooded with the buttery, cheesy tang of Ackerman's. He smiled at the familiar corkscrews of orange inside. How long had it been since he'd pigged out on cheese curls? High school?

He took his time on the short walk back to the courthouse, his thoughts slowed and contemplative. He'd been drifting for a couple of days now, ever since the rendezvous with Cat on the dock. Forty-eight hours, more or less, and nothing had made sense since.

He reached the courthouse with the awareness that the seasons had changed without his even knowing it. It was spring. Cherry trees were budding and the weather was unusually balmy. There wasn't much point in his going back to the office, he realized. He hadn't been worth a damn for the past two days, and today wasn't going to be any different.

He sat on the steps and finished off the cheese puffs, oblivious of the stares and the buzzing of passersby. His mind was elsewhere, floating on a sparkling bay of water. He crumpled the empty bag and watched it slowly spring back to life in his opening hand. The yellow cellophane glimmered like sunshine, and in the mist of his unfocused gaze, he saw a woman with a sad mouth and a lush body.

Sad . . . lush . . . Lord, a man could go crazy.

Breezes stirred, murmurous, cooling the warmth that rose from his skin. She invoked imperatives, that woman. A man had to touch her. He had to have her.

Every aspect of her face drew attention to itself: dark eyebrows feathered with soft strokes of melancholy, sharp cheekbones, and red, ripe lips. She wasn't beautiful. She was feral and haunted and agonizingly lovely. With one wistful glance she could break a mortal man's heart and snuff out his spirit.

Blake wasn't sure when he realized what the woman in his fantasy was doing. Her eyes were hypnotically fixed on the glassy expanse of water, but her hands were performing a slow and lyrical striptease. Alone in the sunshine, luminous, she released one button after another, and each flick of her fingers took a lifetime.

Her clothes drifted to her feet.

Sunlight sheened her breasts.

She dove into the bay, a silver missile streaming through the darkness. He reached out, and as she broke the water and touched his hand, he was naked too. Naked. Aroused. Instantly hard as the water took him into its depths. Achingly hard as she took him into her body. They rolled and spiraled together, and he moved powerfully inside her as the sea pommeled him and dragged at the rhythm of his thrusts.

He would willingly have drowned in exchange for the ecstasy. She wanted it, too, deeper, harder, faster. Red fingernails raked his back as she whimpered in sweet agony . . .

She invoked imperatives, that woman. A man had to have her . . . *even if it destroyed him.*

"Blake?"

The woman called his name twice more before he

looked up and saw Linda standing above him. For a minute he thought she was a figment of his imagination too.

"What are you doing here?" she asked, then she stepped back and scrutinized him. "Wait a minute. What's wrong with this picture? I know, teacher! Blake Wheeler is daydreaming!" She frowned at him. "You are daydreaming, aren't you?"

Blake flipped the Ackerman's bag into a nearby trash receptacle. "Call the guys with the butterfly nets. Wheeler's daydreaming," he said sarcastically.

Linda ticked a finger at him, not about to be put off. "Do you have any idea how long you've been sitting on these steps staring off into space?"

"Not a clue."

"Well, I don't either, but I've been watching you for at least five minutes. I couldn't take my eyes off you, Blake. You looked like a fifteen-year-old kid with a bad case of spring fever."

"Or maybe a thirty-six-year-old DA?"

She crouched and stared into his eyes. "Who is it? The hellcat?"

Blake laughed. "I wouldn't call her that to her face, if I were you."

"You're not me, thank goodness. I wouldn't do anything so foolish as falling in love with a high-strung ex-con."

"Linda."

"Well, I wouldn't."

"Who said anything about love."

"What is it then? Lust?"

Blake rose, mostly to take advantage of the fact that at six feet plus, he towered over his diminutive ex-wife. "Maybe it's like, Linda. Maybe I *like* the woman."

"Umm, right, the way I like Patrick Swayze." She stepped back to size him up. "What's going on, Blake? What do you want from her? Because if it's just sex, forget it. She's not worth the risk to your career, or your political future."

Blake started down the steps.

"Where are you going?" Linda called after him. "It's not even noon yet."

"I've got some things to do."

"Blake!" She sounded worried. "Are you sure you know what you're doing?"

"I know exactly what I'm doing," he said, more to himself than to her. And for the first time in two days, he did. Linda had reminded him of something that had happened on the dock. A question Cat D'Angelo had asked in her soft, desperate voice. *What do you want from me?*

He hadn't answered her then. Now he could because he knew exactly what he wanted from her. It wasn't a burning desire, it was a burning certainty.

"Lemme try it again!" Bumper squealed as he tucked his prized German agate marble, a gift from Cat, into the crook of his index finger and flicked it with his thumb. His "aggie" missed the circle altogether and clinked against a Ginger Bear "glassie" in the stockpile that Cat had accumulated.

He beamed up at Cat. "Howuzzat?" he asked.

"You're getting close, Bumper, mighty close."

Cat turned and winked at Johnny, who was sitting on the steps of the center, watching them both with the amused superiority of a teenager who'd long ago forsaken marbles, aggies or otherwise, for the more manly pursuits.

"You must never discount the game of marbles," Cat told Bumper soberly. "It's a metaphor for life."

"Megafore?"

"Close, Bumper," Johnny said, "*myyyyytee* close."

Cat shot Johnny a look. "It's a figure of speech," she told Bumper. "For instance, if we said Johnny Drescher's a hockey puck, that would be a metaphor."

Bumper pointed at the teenager and howled. "He *is* a hockey puck!"

"Oh, yeah," Johnny countered good-naturedly,

"well, put this in your metaphor pipe and smoke it. Cat D'Angelo walks like a turkey swims." He pointed at Cat's black-and-blue toe, which had turned out to be sprained rather than broken.

"That's a *simile*, Johnny . . . sort of."

"Whatever." Johnny sprawled against the steps, grinning, while Bumper dissolved in gales of laughter.

Cat's little English lesson prompted a great many more metaphors and similes before she could get the two boys calmed down and back to the business of marbles. In fact, she was so busy refereeing the free-for-all, she didn't see the blue Corvette that pulled up across the street and parked.

"Johnny Drescher's a dirty germ!" Bumper squealed, rolling and clutching his sides.

The youngster was obviously getting punchy, Cat realized, wishing she'd never started the "metaphor" game. She held up one of her own aggies as an enticement. "One more shot, okay, Bumper? Just one more? How 'bout it?"

They all glanced up as Blake Wheeler strode down the driveway toward them, his hair wind-tossed and golden, his coat thrown carelessly over his shoulders. He certainly had mastered the casual look, Cat thought. He looked almost poetically disheveled.

"Who's he?" Bumper asked.

"Mr. Wheeler is the district attorney," Cat said.

"Wheeler's a hockey puck!" Bumper exploded.

Even Cat chuckled at that one as she struggled to her feet.

"Interesting mouth on that kid," Blake said, coming up to them. He glanced from Bumper's giggling antics to Cat. "What are you training here, gag writers?"

"Can I help you?" Cat kept her voice cool and professional. Besides the fact that he looked a bit stressed—and she had something to prove—there were two formative young minds watching.

"Let's talk, Cat," he said, wasting no words. "I mean actually talk this time."

"I don't think so."

"Why not?"

"I'm tutoring these boys." *And I'd rather roller-skate down Main Street naked on the Fourth of July than be alone with you again!*

"Tutoring them in marbles?"

"Marbles are a megafore for life," Bumper said.

Blake snuck him a smile and turned back to Cat. "You can't take five minutes?" he asked her, raking a hand through his tousled hair.

Cat shook her head and realized she was enjoying this. Cameron Bay's DA looked positively antsy.

"Five minutes," he pressed. "It's important."

"Shoot for it," Johnny Drescher broke in. He sauntered over to them and scooped up a marble. "If Cat can hit this with an eye-drop," he said, addressing the challenge to Blake, "you clear out. If she can't, you got five minutes to talk."

Cat was about to remind Johnny of his manners, but Blake didn't seem to mind in the least. He rubbed his chin with the look of a shrewd, if faintly desperate, strategist, and considered Johnny's marble. " 'Eye-drop'?"

Johnny placed his marble on the ground and drew a line in front of it. "She stands here and drops her aggie from five feet minimum."

Blake snorted and shook his head. "Never gonna happen."

Cat blanched. He thought she couldn't hit an eye-drop at five feet? "Wait a minute, wait a minute!" she said, refusing to be drawn into the competitive male posturing. "This is not the way adults solve a dispute."

"Yeah? How do adults solve a dispute?" Johnny asked.

Aware of Johnny's skepticism and Bumper's innocent gaze, Cat was determined to demonstrate the spirit of cooperation in action. "Mr. Wheeler and I will compromise. We'll talk. For two and a half minutes." Her smile said, see, even the most antagonistic adults can find common ground. "How does that sound, Mr. Wheeler?"

He smiled back at her, a shade too amused. "Works for me."

She resisted the urge to smack him one as she realized he'd gotten exactly what he wanted. "Johnny," she said, "why don't you walk Bumper home? Would you do that?"

The boys wandered off, Bumper's voice trailing back. "Aw shoot," he said to the older boy, "I thought they were going to have a fight, didn't you, Johnny?"

At least Blake had the decency to wait until the kids were out of earshot before he made reference to the marble on the ground. "Couldn't hit it with a bowling ball," he said.

Cat bristled. "At five feet? In my sleep."

A moment later, her deadeye reputation at stake, she positioned herself over the target. With her biggest marble, a Bumboozer, poised like a bomb between her thumb and forefinger, she closed one eye and took a steadying breath. She was zeroing in on the target like submarine sonar when her injured toe protested. Pain shot through her foot. Wincing, she released the Bumboozer. Too soon!

She squeezed her eyes shut and moaned.

Blake's howl of surprise jolted her. When she opened her eyes, the target marble was spinning madly down the driveway. She'd struck gold!

"How'd you do that?" he demanded.

Barely able to conceal her triumph, she smiled at him and shrugged, a woman to be reckoned with. "Let's talk," she said. "You've got two and a half minutes, and the clock is ticking."

They ended up in the backyard of the center where a small orchard of apple trees was in blossom and hummingbirds hovered breathlessly at feeders.

"What was so important?" she asked him.

"Two days ago, on the dock—"

Cat turned away, her chest suddenly tight. "I'd rather not talk about that."

"You asked me a question," he said, "and I didn't answer it. I want to now." He exhaled and the hesitation took on a sudden, stunning intimacy. "You asked me what I wanted from you."

Cat may have wanted an answer then, but she most definitely did not want one now. "I take the question back."

"Cat, we're not playing marbles now." He reached out and smoothed an errant wisp of her hair into place. "Let me tell you what I want."

Cat braced herself as though for a blow.

"The annual Chamber of Commerce picnic? It's this Sunday. Will you go with me?"

"Picnic . . . ?" She whirled and gaped at him, astonished.

Seven

"Hmmm . . ." Cat pressed her lips together, deliberating as she scrutinized her outfit in the mirror. The dotted Swiss sundress was one of her favorites, but it was probably too dressy for a picnic with horseshoes and watermelon wedges and troops of marauding ants.

She began rummaging through her closet again and came out with seersucker shorts and a matching halter top that had a fifties, Betty Grableish look. This might work, she thought, reaching behind her to unzip the sundress. She stopped as her fingers touched the zipper and sighed tautly, almost laughing. She had no idea why she'd been trying on clothes all morning as though she were actually going to the picnic. She most definitely *wasn't*.

She'd called Blake's office the day after he'd asked her and left a message with his secretary that she couldn't make it. After deliberating all night, she'd finally decided that she just couldn't "date" Blake Wheeler. There was too much unresolved between them—professional issues, personal feelings.

Gwen had argued with her, but finally, when it was clear that Cat couldn't be budged, Gwen had conceded with a suggestion that Cat ought to put in an appearance at the picnic even if she didn't go with Blake. "It's your chance to reintroduce your-self," she'd insisted. "You're going to have to let the town know you're back eventually, dear. You can't hang out here at the center forever."

But Cat wasn't any more ready for reintroductions than she was for dates. She wasn't going, with Blake or otherwise. Her phone message to his secretary ought to have put the issue out of her mind, but it hadn't. Quite the opposite, she'd caught herself daydreaming about the picnic frequently, even planning for it.

The shorts outfit, once she had it on, looked stunning. The flared cut of the shorts lengthened her already long legs and smoothed the lines of her midriff, while the halter top accentuated the soft curves that swelled above it. She even let her hair down and shook it full and thick with her hands. When she was done, the mirror gave her a solid nine. "Whew," she said, breathing the next word that came to mind, "sexy."

She turned away to take the outfit off, then glanced over her shoulder at the mirror and caught her own wry smile. "You're going to the damn picnic, aren't you, D'Angelo?"

The annual Chamber of Commerce picnic was an event that brought the citizenry out en masse. With the exceptions of the Snowflake Charity Ball at Christmas and the Art Foundation dinner, it was the most festive occasion of the year.

Cat knew the day was going to be something of an emotional ordeal as soon as she caught a whiff of Bessie's Broasted Chicken. Bessie's was a local café that provided the food, and the rich, spicy aroma of their spit-broiled chicken filled her nostrils as she pulled her convertible into the parking lot of Mariner's Park.

A smile touched her lips as she walked through the evergreens to the picnic area. She could hear the clinks of tossed horseshoes in the near distance, and the laughter of the players. It had been her dad's favorite game. In those days the Wheeler mill had sponsored the picnic and the highlights had included log-rolling contests on the bay, tree-topping, and ax-throwing. A kind of sadness tugged at Cat as she thought about how much she'd loved the picnic as a child. She'd counted days the whole year.

Bessie's had supplied all the food in those days, too, and now, as Cat approached the "mess tent," she was tantalized by the delicious smells. Whole chickens turned over huge barbecue pits and crocks of potato salad cooled in ice chests. Beer and soda pop flowed from spigots, and coffee simmered in stainless steel urns. Aromas mixed and mingled— corn on the cob, wild blackberry pie, and barrels of briny dill pickles. The sights and smells were heavenly, and for Cat, pure nostalgia.

She found herself looking for Blake as she wandered through the picnic grounds. Mariner's was the most beautiful park in Cameron Bay. Its rolling green belts were dotted with rustic picnic tables, and beyond the picnic area a steamy waterfall fed into a cascading white-water river. There were swarms of people everywhere, some in obvious family groupings, some paired with friends or sweethearts, but she saw no sign of a tall, impossibly handsome DA with roughly the appearance of a sun god.

A baseball game was going strong in the park's diamond as she approached. Cameron Bay and its sister city across the sound were vying for some kind of championship, according to a sign posted on the announcer's booth. The fans were so boisterous, Cat decided to hang around for a while and watch.

A roar went up as the next batter came to the plate. He pulled off his cap and shook his golden hair free, and Cat saw immediately the reason for all the commotion. Blake Wheeler acknowledged the crowd's screams with a quick wave before combing back the sexy tumble of hair with his hands and replacing the cap. His features went taut with concentration as he picked out a bat and readied himself for the task at hand.

Cat watched with avid fascination and some surprise. This was a side of Blake she hadn't known existed. She'd never thought of him as a team player. Must be good for the political image, she decided, and then tweaked herself for being cynical. He looked sincere enough. In fact, he looked downright single-minded.

He tested his bat with a couple of swings while the crowd went wild. They obviously loved him, and Cat could see why. He was something to behold out there on the field. She was struck by his physical presence, and though she'd never been one to dwell on the details of male anatomy, she was dwelling now. His hands she'd noticed before. Good hands, big. But his shoulders were something, too, wide and powerful, muscles rippling through gray cotton jersey as he test-swung the bat. Given the nature of his work, Cat had always credited him with analytical savvy, but she'd never thought of him in terms of physical prowess. She would from now on, undoubtedly.

As he knocked the dirt from his cleats and positioned himself at the plate, Cat heard female wolf whistles. She smiled at their enthusiasm and at that moment probably even shared it. Giving in to an irresistible impulse, she let her eyes brush over the length of him—and regretted it instantly. He was built big everywhere it counted, and where it didn't count, he was narrow and breathtakingly solid. Jersey pants encased his thighs, and from where Cat was standing, she could see they were hugging the rest of him as well. Of course the crowd loved him. His sex appeal was blinding, and yet he seemed to symbolize everything good and strong and rugged about the sport. That is the magic of Blake Wheeler, she decided. He gave them boy-next-door and lusty male sexuality all wrapped up in one package.

The bat-testing ritual over, Blake nodded to the pitcher and bent forward, poised to smash one out of the park. The slight shifting of his hips was a reflex, but it nearly wrecked Cat's heart. Not a bump and grind exactly, but the movement was wildly sensual nonetheless. She found herself fixated, waiting for him to do it again.

The crack of his bat brought her back to the game. She was just in time to see him blast the ball into left field. It was a powerful line drive that scorched the short stop's glove as he flung himself at the ball and missed it.

Blake surged toward first base, rigid muscles now fluidly in motion. He rounded the bag, his face taut as he gauged his chances, made a decision, and sprinted for second. He dove just as the second baseman leapt in the air to catch the ball.

Blake disappeared in a cloud of flying dust, and the crowd went nuts. The baseman overextended, a split-second miscalculation that caused the ball to ricochet off the heel of his glove. He hit the ground off-balance, flailing and cursing.

Blake materialized out of the dust storm, sprinting for third. The crowd roared. The scrambling second baseman got his hands on the ball and jackknifed it to third.

As the third baseman ran out for the throw, his eyes fixed on the ball, he made the fatal error of veering into the path of an oncoming tornado. Blake hit the man like a semi without brakes. The collision was bone crunching. Both men went down.

Cat heard herself gasp with the crowd.

She ran to the Cyclone fence and called Blake's name, unable to see him as the other players crowded around. Cat clung to the steel chain links, waiting for the sound of sirens as the security guards mobilized to keep the spectators off the field.

Finally the cluster parted, and she could see that

Blake was standing. He was roughed up and his jersey was torn, but he seemed to be in one piece as he dusted himself off and grinned. He obviously hadn't heard her calling him over the noise of the crowd. She was almost as grateful for that as for the fact that he wasn't hurt. The third baseman appeared then, shaken, but still intact. The onlookers whistled and howled and generally created pandemonium.

A moment later, the game announcer risked his life when he gave the crowd the bad news. Blake had been thrown out at third. The booing, hissing, and foot-stomping that resulted was thunderous. Blake did his best to calm the furor, but the mood was explosive. Finally he grabbed the coach's bullhorn and climbed the Cyclone fence, calling out to the stands, "We can still win! Hang 'em high!"

It was the team's battle cry, and it worked. The noise leveled off momentarily, then the cheer went up: "Hang 'em high!"

Cat yelled right along with them. The fervor had caught her, stirring her blood until she felt as rowdy and electrified as the crowd. "Hang 'em high!" she shouted, jumping up and down, her voice cracking. That's when it hit her what she was doing.

Much to her relief no one seemed to have spotted her, including the wounded warrior who was hanging on the fence less than ten feet away. He was the antithesis of the ruthless courtroom lawyer she remembered. He looked dog tired, was sheened with sweat, and a huge smudge of dirt decorated his jaw.

If I didn't know who he was, she thought, smiling ruefully, *I'd be in love.*

He noticed her as he jumped down to the ground. He didn't say anything. He just stared at her as though he couldn't quite believe his eyes. That was when she saw that his lip was bleeding, just a little. His lower lip. She could discern a tiny, jagged rent in its fullness and a slash of crimson that made her throat tighten.

She touched her own lips automatically, and her neck went hot as fire. What was she doing?

He smiled faintly, and Cat stepped back from the fence, her heart pounding. She was instantly afraid that she might have given something away, although she wasn't sure what it would have been. She just didn't want to do anything that could be construed as—interest.

He brushed a finger along his lower lip and held the finger back, staring at the blood. When he looked up at her, there was something different in his eyes: a sharpening of focus that was silver-flecked and enigmatic. It was almost as though he knew something about her. Something he hadn't known before.

Cat had the oddest sensation that the ground was shifting under her feet. They weren't close enough to touch or even to talk, but something was happening between them, and it was almost as physical as the breeze blowing her hair. A sparkle of energy filled the pit of her stomach. Cat caught her breath as it brightened inside her, glittering like a multifaceted crystal. Within seconds the sharpening sensations had forced her to look away—at her dusty sandaled feet, at anything but him!

This is silly, she thought, this is ridiculous. But a smile warmed nervously on her lips. She could feel his eyes on her. She could feel the energy flow connecting them, and it was as intimate as anything she'd ever experienced.

She was also aware that some of Blake's teammates had begun to notice what was going on. Even the crowd in the stands had grown quieter. She glanced around, cutting a small, quick arc with her head. Did Blake realize that people were staring at them? He looked as though he couldn't care less. He looked as though he were going to rip off his jersey and come after her any second!

That was it for Cat, the end of the line. Somebody had to stop the craziness. Stiff at the joints, and without knowing where she was going, she turned and walked away from the stands.

Moments later she was in Bessie's tent filling a plate with baked beans and potato salad and corn, and hoping against hope that food would settle her down. Carbohydrates were nature's tranquilizers, she told herself. She found a relatively isolated spot near an empty coffee urn and parked herself there, picking at her baked beans and glancing up every time someone entered the tent.

Fixing a smile on her face, she checked out the room as though she were waiting for someone. She *was* half-expecting Blake to show up now that he'd seen her. She imagined trying to explain to him what she was doing at the picnic and couldn't come up with anything that sounded remotely sensible. In fact, she realized, if she were going to start being sensible at this late point, she should finish her food and leave.

But she didn't leave. And he didn't seek her out.

Cheering noises outside the tent finally prompted Cat to leave her sanctuary. A laughing throng was gathered on the picnic grounds where a heavy-set man in a clown suit with a "Mr. Stitches" button was juggling apples, doing an Irish jig, and generally acting nonsensical.

The clown completed the juggling sequence, flipped one of the apples over his head, and swung around as Cat caught it. She tossed it back to him, and the crowd applauded.

"A big hand for my assistant!" he said, grabbing Cat's hand and pulling her into the circle.

Cat laughed and gently tried to extricate herself, to no avail. Mr. Stitches had no intention of letting her go.

"Now the fun begins!" he shouted to the crowd. "Pair up for the three-legged races!" He bent toward Cat. "What's your name, sugar?"

"Cat," she said, "but—"

"Let's get this beautiful lady a partner! Whaddaya say, fellas? Who wants to be tied up to Cat?"

"Yo!" several men shouted. Hands went up. Whistles and shouts sailed up like last year's fireworks.

"No, really, I can't," Cat said, straining to be heard above the clamor. "I sprained my toe." She pointed to her foot, but nobody seemed to care about her faintly purple digit. A smattering of applause broke out, which Cat thought was for her at first.

"Look who's here!" Mr. Stitches said, spotting someone in the crowd. "Darn if it isn't our star baseball player. Bruised and bloodied, but unbeaten, right, Blake? Get on out here!"

The applause built, and Cat craned her neck to see where their star baseball player was. Blake finally materialized through the crowd, looking slightly embarrassed over the fuss. The female wolf whistles started all over again as the crowd laid their eyes on him. This time the reaction seemed prompted largely by the fact that he'd pulled off his torn jersey and tied it around his waist.

Cat saw immediately that her brief flight of fancy during the game hadn't done him justice. The muscle definition of his upper body was worthy of calendar art. Golden hair whorled over his pecs, and the darker diamond on his abdomen crept sensually toward his gray jersey pants. It was only with the greatest difficulty that Cat was able to bring her thoughts above the belt. And even as she did, heat flashed up her neck to her scalp.

The clown held up Cat's hand as though he were about to auction her off. "This sweet young thing needs a partner for the three-legged race," he said. "You up for that, Blake?"

"Up for it?" Blake smiled.

Cat died a thousand deaths. "My toe," she said.

The clown bustled Blake up front and dropped him next to Cat, then deserted them both to go off in search of more three-legged racers.

"You're going to regret this," Cat whispered to Blake. "I can barely navigate on two legs."

Blake shot her a quick grin. "You're talking to the guy who plays baseball on his face."

His eyes sparkled in the sunlight, full of male mischief, and Cat nearly got lost in the breath she was taking. This was a bad dream, of course. Like Pam Ewing in *Dallas*, she would wake up any minute now. She had to, because it was beyond comprehension that Cat D'Angelo was about to be bound to Blake Wheeler from ankle to thigh!

"Relax," Blake suggested as Mr. Stitches returned with several more hapless couples, "this could be fun."

"Fun for who?" Cat murmured darkly.

"Here's your rope," the clown said, passing out soft white cords to each pair. "Go tie yourselves up." Cat knew better than to say what came to mind as Blake turned to her. His expression suggested he was employing restraint as well. There would be no more bondage jokes.

They found a quiet spot and avoided each other's eyes for an awkward moment or two. Blake fingered the ropes in his hand. "I guess we'd better do this," he said.

"Yes, I guess we'd better." Cat took the initiative and went to stand alongside him. Pressing her leg to his, she felt the warmth of him immediately. It penetrated the jersey fabric of his pants along with another sensation, the soft prickle of his body hair. That's when they discovered her hips were half a foot lower than his. "We don't fit," she said.

Blake's quiet smile said he wasn't going to touch that line either. "Sit down," he suggested. "Let's try it that way."

Resolving not to say another word, Cat sank down next to him on the grass. An uneasy silence prevailed as Blake tied a cord around their ankles first. Even he seemed to realize there was no possibility for safe conversation.

He hesitated with the next cord, and Cat realized

he was waiting for her to open her legs. He was going to tie their thighs together! "Do you have to?" she asked.

"Have you even run a three-legged race?"

She must have, but she couldn't remember it.

"I have to," was all he said.

She drew her leg up, forcing him to draw his up, too. "Proceed." She sounded like someone who'd just finished her last cigarette and was facing the firing squad.

He proceeded, his fingers brushing her leg in ways that made her feel dizzy. He seemed to be taking care not to touch anything he shouldn't, but the soft friction of his skin against the inside of her thigh was wildly suggestive nonetheless. Muscles tightened automatically, but the sensation inside her was anything but tight. It was pooling warmth and darts of light. She was melting like the butter dripping off Bessie's corn! Somehow she resisted the urge to squirm. It wasn't until he'd finished that she realized she could have tied the ropes herself. She had two hands!

The rope-tying was the least of it, Cat realized as they faced their next challenge: standing up. They managed it finally, but not without getting embarrassingly experimental. By the time they were upright, Cat had discovered that the hair under his arms was reddish gold and that he had a sexy little mole near his fifth rib. She didn't want to think what he might have learned about her!

"This is a crime against nature," she said half-seriously as they were struggling to get back to the picnic area moments later. "People weren't meant to tie their bodies together for the entertainment of others."

Blake might have agreed with her except that their tied bodies were entertaining him immensely. She was forced to cling to him to keep from falling, and the soft crush of her breasts against his ribs was arousing his pulse beat, among other things. Every awkward attempt at navigation crowded her breasts into a soft shimmer of décolletage. To a man who'd never seen her in anything but buttoned-up-to-the-chin blouses, it was the sensual equivalent of Disneyland.

Their appearance brought a rousing cheer from the spectators as they arrived at the start line. Blake gave Cat a few pointers while the clown organized the other racers. "Start with your free leg first," he told her, "then swing out the tied leg—and *hang* on to me. Got that?"

Cat nodded. Free leg first. Swing out. *Hang on to him.* When the whistle blew, she gave it everything she had.

By some miracle, they surged off the starting block together and chugged down the course like a well-oiled machine. Pounding, panting, gripping each other fiercely, they were one mind, one goal. They were actually pulling into the lead when Cat rocked down on something hard with her sprained toe. Not again! she thought as pain rocketed through her foot. She moaned and lurched forward.

"Hang on to me!" Blake shouted.

She clung to him as he lifted her right off the ground, hauling her with him for several seconds before gravity and forward momentum got the best of them. They went down like acrobats, rolling and tumbling like loose logs.

"Heads!" someone bellowed as spectators leapt out of their way. Fortunately for everyone concerned, the thick green grass made a perfect tumbling mat. Blake and Cat ended up in a heap near a refuse barrel, their ropes untied except for the ankle cords.

They were instantly surrounded by concerned spectators. One teenage wise guy suggested CPR, his eyes on Cat. Someone else wanted to call an ambulance.

"We're fine," Blake assured everyone. "Really, go back to the race." Finally, at his insistence, the crowd dispersed to cheer on the winners.

"*Are* you okay?" Blake asked, staring down at the

gasping woman beneath him. She was flat on her back, and he felt a twitch of concern when she couldn't seem to catch her breath.

"Can you move your toes?" he asked.

"M-maybe," she got out, ". . . with help."

That's when he realized she was laughing, a soft squeak of a sound that made him want to gather her up and kiss her. It was the sexiest laughter he'd ever heard. It was breathy and infectious, with a husky quaver that made the hair on his arms stand up. Kiss her, hell, he wanted to roll around in the grass with her and make passionate love to her right there in the park. Pleasure knotted inside him, intense and then diffuse. He could feel the heat in his groin, the pressure. And then another sensation welled up with it . . . laughter.

"Told you I couldn't navigate," she said, breathless.

"That's true, but you hang on good."

With some effort they eventually got themselves calmed down, untied, and retired to the shade of a maple tree.

"Blew the baseball game *and* the three-legged race," Blake said, rolling onto his back to stare up at the sky. "My political career is over before it's started."

"Bet you never thought it would be me who'd bring you down." Cat plucked yellow fuzz off a dandelion and avoided his eyes.

"Sure I did. It had to be you."

Her fingers stilled on the flower. "Great little song title," she said. She stared at the dandelion until finally she had no choice but to look at him. He was gazing at her like a man with something unspeakably sexy on his mind.

"Why do you say things like that to me?" she asked. "Why do you look at me like that?"

"Like what?"

"Intimately."

"Is it a problem?"

"*Yes*, it's a problem. We're not even friends, Blake."

"Right"—his voice cracked slightly—"we've got to do something about that."

She held off for a long time in the hope that her breathing would return to some sort of normalcy. "Is that what you want then? To be friends?"

"No, not just friends . . . lovers."

Cat dropped the flower.

He rolled to his side, propped a fist against his jaw, and gazed at her intently. There was enough wattage in his eyes to singe the clothing off her body. Cat caught her breath. Her voice was a whisper. "You can't talk to me like that."

"How would you like me to talk to you?"

"Normally, for heaven's sake."

"That's a tall order." He picked up the flower and plucked at it slowly—she loves me, she loves me not. "Can I ask you a question?"

"Yes, a normal question."

He plucked one last petal and smiled at her. "Are you angry at me because *I* want us to be lovers? Or because *you* want it?"

"I don't want it—"

Instantaneously Cat's body made a liar out of her. Her pulse ripped out of control, and her throat went dry as cotton. Her internal thermostat was going crazy! She was hot on the inside and cold on the outside. Everything felt shuddery and steamy inside, and she was damp in embarrassing places.

She pressed a hand to her throat and felt the truth of her burning flesh, her stitching pulse. All right, yes! She *did* want to be with him. She wanted his huge hands all over her! She wanted to do all the unspeakably sexy things his eyes suggested.

"There may be things I want," she said at last, her voice shaking like water. "But I don't have to like wanting them."

"Is one of them me?"

She hugged her legs to her chest and mumbled something into her knees.

"Was that a yes?"

Her headshake said no. But his fingers caught her chin and drew her face around to him. His eyes were so incandescently silver, she could hardly look at him. "What if it was?" she said.

"Say it. Let me hear you say it."

"No."

"Say it, Cat," he said. "Don't drive me out of my mind."

There was something taut and male and obsessive in his voice. It frightened her. It thrilled her and sliced through her self-control like a gleaming knife blade. She whispered the word he wanted to hear and felt his hands tremble slightly on her face. Before she could breathe, he was in front of her, kneeling, holding her shoulders.

He stared into her eyes a long time. "Let's get out of here," he said.

"No . . . I can't do this so quickly."

"All right then, soon. There's a party for the center this Friday, a fund-raiser at the community center. Let me take you there."

"I don't think so—"

"Then I'll take you home afterward. I'll do it any way you want it, but I want you with me. That's as long as I can wait for you, Cat. I won't make it past Friday."

He was desperate, and a little wild. The very idea of Blake Wheeler's needing anything that badly astonished her. It startled her lips into a smile. "Have you gone crazy?"

"Crazy?" He considered the possibility. "No, this feels like one of the saner things I've done in a while."

He *was* crazy, she thought, her heart rocketing. Her skin registered the heat of his hands, the iron will of his fingers, and she knew in her heart that it was all over. She had lost the fight, if that's what it was. She didn't know how or when or where it would happen between them, but it *was* going to happen.

Eight

Cat had never prepared with such feverish intensity for anything in her life. She scooped her hair up, took it down, pinned one side back, considered ironing out the curl, and even toyed with the idea of tinting it another color. I'm crazed, she thought, bobby pins poking out of her mouth as she stared at herself in the bathroom vanity. She rescued the drooping strap of her teddy and removed the pins from her mouth before she accidentally swallowed one. Maybe a side part with a Lauren Bacall pageboy? She actually wanted to look sexy and desirable tonight, and she hadn't wanted to do that for a man in years.

She tried the side part and blew hair out of her eyes. *Too* sexy, she decided, it had to go back up. She began pinning again with the sneaking suspicion that all the frantic activity might be a way to keep her from thinking too much about the evening ahead. Even Gwen had been startled when Cat told her the news. "You're going to the fund-raiser with Blake? You two certainly mended the fences quickly!"

Cat's head was swimming with the suddenness of it all. She felt like a body surfer caught in a riptide with no recourse but to ride out the dangerous current. She didn't understand the forces working on

106

her, but they were powerful. It had something to do with Blake's belief that they had to be together. He was irresistible in his certainty, as spellbinding as a prophet. And she seemed nearly helpless in the face of it.

But there were other factors, too, the most significant of which was her honesty about her feelings after all these years. She'd been in love with him once, puppy love, but what she felt now had that same fierce quality of longing.

She stared into her own eyes and asked the question forming in her mind. The answer came back on a flash of panic. No way! She was *not* in love with him. That was absurd. She couldn't be in love with someone she'd virtually hated for the past ten years. And yet she knew about love and hate, about their interchangeability. Emotions were quixotic things that could transform on you in a flash. She was confused, she was sure of that if nothing else. There was so much turbulence inside her—edgy, riveting sensations that had as much to do with fear as they did with sexual attraction.

Cat still wasn't ready for her "date" two hours later when the doorbell rang. She was burying one last hairpin in the magnificent mop of mahogany she'd piled on top of her head.

"I'm coming!" she called, grabbing her high heels off the bed. She tried to get them on as she dashed for the door, and her run-and-hop gait shook several strategically placed hairpins loose. Passing the clock mirror in the hallway, she caught a look at herself. A wild woman on the run. Swell, she thought, slipping on the last shoe as she clutched the door handle. She'd wanted to look cool and beautiful and sophisticated when she opened the door.

What Blake saw when Cat opened the door was a bombshell. She was flushed pink with excitement and dark curls were flying every which way. The oversized cowl neckline of her dress had drooped off one shoulder, and her hemline was hiked up on one sleek thigh. She looked like a woman who, if she hadn't just come from a man's bed, ought to be heading there directly.

Blake thought that was the best idea he'd had all day.

Cat thought he was one of the stormiest, sexiest men she'd ever laid eyes on. Every time she saw him, he was more compelling in some indefinable way. This time it was his gray eyes with their mesmerizing darts of quicksilver. And his mouth! Along with the tiny laceration, the set of his mouth held a message that Cat tried to decipher with the quickening beats of her heart. It was about how much he wanted her—and how there was going to be hell to pay if he didn't get what he wanted.

"Do I get to come in?" he asked.

She stepped back and felt the wake of his energy field as he walked past her. *Lord, I'll bet he's a tiger in the sack,* she thought, then felt her neck go steamy red. What was the matter with her?

He turned as soon as she shut the door, his voice low and sexy. "I don't care if we ever get to that fund-raiser, do you?"

"Not go?" Her hands wobbled as she tried to reinsert a dangling hairpin. "Well, I—I really ought to put in an appearance. It is for the center. And you— aren't you supposed to say a few words, or something?"

"How about if I say them to you instead . . ." He walked to her and slowly took the hairpin from her hand, then he pulled another from her hair and another . . . until a breathtaking swirl of mahogany tumbled around her face.

"Give all your money to the youth center, folks," he said, his voice husky, "because it has a beautiful counselor-in-training who believes in kids and shoots marbles. And because she looks so deliciously half-disheveled right now that I want to finish the job . . ."

He hesitated, curving his palm to her throat. Cat

felt her legs go weak as he rode her lower lip with his thumb, just as he'd done on the dock. It was poetry, his touch. *Erotic* poetry. It shocked the senses and aroused the nerves.

". . . in bed." His jaw muscles tautened and his thumb bit sweetly into the softness of her lip. "Let me take you to bed, Cat," he said, his eyes flashing irresistibly. "Let me take you and take you . . . until you're soft and wet and sighing from the bliss."

He brought her fingers to his lips and kissed their trembling tips. And then he drew her forefinger into his mouth just long enough to make it warm and wet. "Let me take you like this," he said, "slowly, tenderly."

Cat fell up against the wall, limp as a baby. She was speechless with shock, immobilized. Her heart hammered inside her like some crazy intruder, and the gush of desire in her depths drained the strength right out of her body. Seconds later, as she looked up at him, there was a kind of pain in her facial muscles. It was need, she realized, pure, unadulterated physical need.

"There you go again," she said, pressing her fingers to her throat, "rushing things."

He smiled quietly. "Yeah, it works, doesn't it?"

She sighed, despair laced with desire. "Blake, we can't do this. We'll never get to the party."

"That's exactly why we have to do it." He brought her fingers to his mouth again and sent a shiver of pleasure through her. "*I* have to do it."

She could so easily have given in to him, in a second, without a whimper of protest. Her fantasies were telling her it would be the most incredible experience of her life. She *wanted* to give in. But she couldn't, not yet. There were doubts in her mind, niggling little concerns that crept back into her awareness whenever he turned off the heat and gave her a moment to breathe. They thrived inside her, those concerns, like a troop of tiny security guards, patrolling, watching, warning her that there were too many unknowns, that he hadn't proved himself yet.

Proved himself . . . ?

"I'm in love with this mouth," he said, his thumb caressing her lip line with a sensitivity that made her stomach clutch. "Crazy about it."

"Blake . . . take me to the party."

"Really?"

"Yes, I'd like to go." I need to go, she thought, staring up at his strong, handsome features. I need you to take me and show me that Blake Wheeler and Cat D'Angelo can be together at a civic function. Suddenly it was crucial that he prove to her that she was good enough for him, that he wanted her with him, right beside him with Cameron Bay's elite looking on. "I think we should, don't you?" It was a test, she realized.

"Sense of duty, huh?" A smile touched his eyes as he tried to look stern. "Okay, but we're not staying long."

She was pleased that he acquiesced so easily, with hardly any hesitation at all. Round one, Wheeler, she thought, smiling back at him radiantly. He had passed with flying colors.

The fund-raiser was in full swing when Blake and Cat got there. Gwen rushed over to greet them, two flutes of champagne in her hand. Cat took hers gratefully.

"How do I look?" Gwen asked, twirling for them. "The old party dress. I took it out of mothballs."

"You look beautiful," Cat assured her, admiring the older woman's graceful carriage and sea-green gown.

Gwen accepted the compliment with a pleased smile. "You, too, sweetheart, *très chic.*"

Apparently Blake agreed. At any rate, he chose that moment to give Cat a look that was hot enough to peel the community center's wallpaper. "Been here long enough?" he murmured.

Cat blushed.

Gwen blinked at them both in surprise. "Uh . . . have fun, kids," she said, excusing herself to welcome some other late arrivals. The hospital auxiliary league was hosting the event, but Gwen, as director of the center, was the official greeter.

Blake pressed his hand to Cat's shoulder blades as though to guide her into the room. Feigning a glance behind them, he gave her a thrill of surprise as he rode his thumb down the track of her zipper. "When do I get to take this dress off you?" he asked, sotto voce.

Cat nearly dropped her evening bag. Her eyes widened as a ripple of shocked pleasure followed the path of his thumb. She shot him a warning glance and fixed a smile on her face. She had enough trouble with her image without having Cameron Bay's DA unzipping her right there in front of everyone. "Behave," she said.

A smile flickered, and Blake took a swallow of his champagne. He unbuttoned his jacket and slipped a hand into his pants pocket. "For now."

Cat breathed a sigh of relief. He seemed to be resigning himself to his white-knight role, if only temporarily. He looked rugged and suave in his double-breasted suit, a man of consequence. Evidence of a heavy beard shadowed his features despite a close shave and his burnished gold hair. He was a handsome, sexy devil, Cat thought, with the emphasis on devil.

With some difficulty Cat turned her attention to the crowd. Everyone of note had arrived, she quickly realized, and no one seemed to have noticed Blake's outrageousness yet. Cat even thought she recognized a couple of fellow classmates from Bayside High as she scanned the crowd for familiar faces.

Sam Delahunt, the mayor, spotted them as they entered the buffet area. "Blake? How are you, son?

We've been expecting you." He strolled toward them, glancing at Cat with open curiosity. "Do I—uh, do I know this young lady?"

"Catherine D'Angelo," Cat said before Blake could speak.

A flicker of recognition crossed Sam's face. "Oh, yes, I believe my daughter, Linda, mentioned you. Vince D'Angelo's daughter?"

"Yes, that's right. I'm up from Berkeley, working at the center this summer."

He arched an eyebrow thoughtfully. "Yes, yes—Johnny Drescher's one of your clients, isn't he? I hope you can talk some sense into that young roughneck."

"Roughneck?" Cat was as startled by the mayor's awareness of her work with Johnny as she was to hear her client referred to in such a manner.

"Excuse us, Sam," Blake said, claiming Cat's arm. "I want to introduce Ms. D'Angelo around."

Blake spirited Cat away. Negotiating Cameron Bay's well-heeled and influential set, he courteously put off any and all guests who attempted to engage him in conversation. Cat was acutely aware of the stares directed at them, and the whispering, but if Blake noticed it, he didn't let on. Moving purposefully, he guided her around potential roadblocks and out onto a terrace redolent of spring lilacs and fresh night air.

Blake found a private corner and drew her into his arms without any preamble whatsoever. "You've got five minutes," he said, lifting her chin. His breath was warm against her mouth, fragrant with champagne.

"For what?"

"To come up with an excuse to get us out of this party."

"What happens when the five minutes are up?"

"I may have to start right here, lady. Have you ever had a district attorney lift your sweet little skirt and take you in a flower bed?"

That time Cat did drop her purse. "You're danger-ous!"

"You've got that right," he said.

"If seduction were a crime, Wheeler, you'd be doing a life sentence."

Their laughter took the edge off Blake's ultimatum, but he had no intention of letting things get too relaxed. He wanted her dizzy and hot and off bal-ance. He wasn't crazy. Not unless sexual urgency was a certifiable condition. He'd never been saner or more laser-focused in his life. He wanted a woman. This woman. Tonight. Her dark eyes and wide, sexy mouth made him knot up with desire. He was tight all over, primed as a twelve-gauge shotgun, to quote one of Sam Delahunt's expressions.

"I'm usually a fairly articulate man, but there aren't too many ways to say this." He drew a finger down her throat, hesitating on the chaotic pulse point. "I'm on fire, lady. And I think you're a little warm yourself."

Her body stiffened deliciously. "I am . . . warm," she admitted, her cheeks aflame.

The twelve-gauge cocked explosively inside Blake. "What are we doing here?"

Cat's heart surged wildly as he caught her hand and led her across the terrace. She went without protest, more convinced than ever that she was the crazy one, not him. He knew what he wanted. She didn't know anything except that she was too weak with colliding desires to fight anymore.

She didn't realize until they reached the front door of the community center that she'd left something lying on the brick floor of the terrace.

"Go on out to the car," she told Blake in a whis-per. "I left my bag. I'll be right there."

The purse was exactly where she'd dropped it. Breathless, she scooped it up and dusted it off. Her heart was pounding so hard she almost didn't hear the murmured comment that drifted through the wrought-iron latticework of a trellis to her left.

"Who the hell is she, anyway?"

It was a hushed question, a man's voice. Curious, Cat peered through the arabesques of the ironwork and noticed the small group of men clustered on the other side. Perhaps it was something about their clandestine manner that alerted her, or the low pitch of their conversation. Whatever it was, she stopped for a moment to listen.

"She's got a record, doesn't she?" one of the men asked.

Cat had never seen him before, but she did know the man who answered. It was Sam Delahunt, the mayor.

"Juvenile," Sam said, "her file has probably been sealed. It was car theft if I remember correctly."

"Car theft?" one of the others scoffed. "What in hell would Blake want with a woman like that?"

A strange sort of immobilization took over Cat's muscles as she realized they were talking about her. She was panicky about being discovered, and even more apprehensive about what she was going to hear, but she couldn't leave until she'd heard it.

Laughter erupted. "What does any man want with a woman like that—a quick tumble."

"This could play hell with our plans for running him next year," Sam muttered. "I'll have a talk with him."

One of the men snorted. "No—let him get it out of his system. She's a hot little number, and he knows it. The boys down at the courthouse have a pool going that he beds her before the week's out."

Cat had stopped breathing seconds before. Now her stomach slid with queasiness.

"You think he'll drop her?" Sam's voice was uncertain.

"Of course," the other man said. "His interest in this D'Angelo woman extends to her body. It's the conquest that turns on Blake Wheeler. That's why he's such a damn good DA, gentlemen."

Male laughter wafted toward Cat in the dimness.

A shudder gripped her, and the next thing she knew she was rushing out the back door of the center, clutching her purse to her stomach and fighting off a rising need to be sick.

The alley she ended up in was steeped in dirty-yellow light from the back windows of the community center. The air was suffocatingly still for a Cameron Bay night, and a pungent muskiness drifting off the bay permeated Cat's nostrils and set off her queasy stomach.

The past welled up, swamping her in shame and helpless fury. All her life she'd felt like cheap goods—the kid from the wrong side of the tracks, the "wild child." Now, with a few whispered words, she'd just been reduced to that vile category again. She couldn't go back inside. She couldn't face those filthy old men, the bastards. Or Blake either.

She stumbled through the alley's loose gravel in her high heels and cut across a vacant lot to the main drag. Music and laughter poured from a passing car. Hurriedly, she began to walk toward the city center. The only thing on her mind was getting home. She was absently aware of buildings as she passed them, the high school and the courthouse, but not of movement. Despite her feverish pace she had the nightmarish feeling of walking and walking and getting nowhere, a treadmill in hell.

She regressed steadily, her thoughts jammed with bitterness and finally self-loathing. Maybe the old bastards were right. Maybe she would ruin Blake's career. Their claim that he was after sex was certainly true. Maybe that was *all* he was after from a "hot little number" like Cat D'Angelo.

Hurt stung through her jaw muscles like acid. One more degradation at the hands of Blake Wheeler. It was becoming a form of self-abuse. Why did she subject herself to it? Did she care so little for her own personal dignity?

Cars passed her infrequently, and she didn't bother

to turn as she heard one pull up to the curb along-side her.

"Cat?" Blake called her name and honked. "What are you doing here? Why did you leave without me?"

She stumbled and swore. "Leave me alone," she said, forcing him to brake as she cut across the street in front of his car. "Just leave me alone, dammit!" She was too full of outrage to deal with him now. She would either rail at him for his contemptibility or blubber like an idiot.

"Cat!"

A horn sounded, and she stopped in the stream of his headlights, confused. She craned around but saw no other traffic. The city park loomed ahead of her, just beyond the curve of the road. It looked dark and impenetrable. She started for it with a vengeance, praying she could disappear in its shadows.

Blake wheeled the car out and pulled up alongside her again, pacing her as she strode up the street. Her hair had come loose on one side and was streaming behind her. The slim dress she wore rode up with the swing of her legs, and there was an awkward, angry grace in the height of her head. She looked like a beautiful, spiteful banshee. But what was she so furious about? he wondered. And where the hell was she going?

Beyond Blake's confusion there was the frustration. Lady, you sure put a kink in the plans for tonight, he thought, glancing at the tight switch and sway of her posterior.

"You can't walk on the streets at this time of night, Cat." He stopped the car and opened his door. "Get in the car."

She shook her head, freeing more mahogany hair from its restraints as she jogged ahead of the car. "I can walk anywhere I want! This is still a free country."

Blake jammed the Corvette into neutral and swung himself out of the bucket seat. "What's going on, Cat?"

"I don't want to talk about it, all right? Leave me alone!"

"Hold up, dammit. Cat!"

He returned to the car, watched her storm off, and without thinking, spiked the gas pedal with his foot. Still in neutral, the Corvette's engine roared and spit fire like an angry dragon, and Blake took unexpected pleasure in the sound. Cat D'Angelo was beginning to make him angry.

Moonlight flashed off her white form as she disappeared into the darkness of the city park. Blake pulled the car to the side of the road and ripped his keys from the ignition. Mariner's was a big park. If he didn't catch up with her quickly, he'd lose her altogether.

He moved silently through the trees, listening for her footfall and catching a glimpse of white here and there. By the time he got a fix on her, she was a wisp of silvery smoke heading across the park toward the waterfall. She made him think of forest nymphs and dryads.

She'd stopped by the river when he caught up with her. He came to a halt several feet away, struck by the sight of her in the iridescent light. Her shoulders were heaving as though she'd been running for her life, and she looked like a frightened deer who might bolt into the river to escape him.

At first he wasn't sure she'd seen him, but she spun around as he approached, her eyes blazing.

"Stay away, Wheeler. I'm warning you."

So much for forest nymphs. She looked angry enough to murder him. "Let's stop playing games, Cat," he said, approaching her. "What the hell is wrong?"

"Games? You want *me* to stop playing games?"

"What's that supposed to mean?"

"It means you're a bastard, Wheeler—like all the rest of them." She whirled and faced the spuming river again, clutching her arms. "It means I *hate* you."

Blake had never witnessed such contained fury in

a woman. She was explosive, shaking from head to toe, and as primed to go off as the stick of dynamite he'd once fantasized.

"I hate you," she whispered again.

This time he heard the catch in her voice. It was a husky break that cut through his frustration long enough to give him a glimpse of her turmoil. In that moment she looked so conflicted he wanted to take her in his arms. She made him burn with needs he didn't understand. Women didn't come any more difficult, and yet he had this outrageous desire to connect with her, to whisper into her hair and gentle the fury shaking through her body.

He walked to where she stood and spoke quietly to her rigid back. "Cat, what is it? Talk to me."

She shook her head, and another ribbon of dark hair tumbled down from its precarious perch on the crown of her head. He felt her stiffen even before he'd smoothed back the cascading hair, but he carried out the impulse anyway.

"Don't!" She jerked away as though his touch repulsed her.

Blake pulled back, stunned. Her shrillness sliced at him. "What the hell is wrong with you?"

She whirled and glared at him. "Maybe I don't like you, Wheeler. Maybe you're one of the biggest bastards around! How's that for a reason?" She shoved past him, jamming an elbow into his ribs in her furious rush to get away.

Blake's grunt of pain was reflexive. His confusion became raw disbelief. Difficult, hell! She was a blazing little witch. Frustration—sexual and every other kind known to man—knotted in his muscles. "You want a bastard?" he called after her. "You've got one, lady."

He closed the distance between them in a few quick strides, caught her by the wrist, and whipped her around. Her gasp didn't stop him, and neither did the quiver of apprehension in her mouth. He'd had enough of her emotional pyrotechnics to last him a lifetime.

"I'm losing patience with the sixteen-year-old delinquent routine, D'Angelo." He breathed the next words through closed teeth. "Grow up, dammit. Or maybe you need a couple more years in Purdy Hall?"

Her face drained of blood, and the sound that came out of her was heart-catching. Blake didn't have time to respond to her distress, or even to register it. She tore free of his hold and slapped him hard, twice, an open-hand crack to his jaw, followed by a stinging backhand. And then she staggered backward, gasping.

Blake's jaw burned like fire as he stared at her. He touched the welling heat where her hand had connected, and colliding urges took shape inside him. He didn't know whether to grab her and shake her until she couldn't breathe—or to beg her forgiveness. Tears sparkled brilliantly in her eyes and her hands were fisted at her mouth.

"What do you want from me?" she whispered, her breath shaking each word. "Haven't you hurt me enough?"

Blake felt as though a truck had rammed him.

"No more," she said, a sob breaking her voice. "No more, Wheeler. Leave me alone."

Hurt and anger glittered in her eyes, but it was the emotion locked up in her mouth that wrenched at Blake. All the years of heartache seemed to be imprisoned there, waiting for someone to set them free, to set her free. Guilt flashed through him, a soft, sharp aching that laid its weight on his muscles like a heavy blanket.

"I'm sorry," he said, not knowing exactly what he meant at that moment, except that he was sorry . . . for everything that had happened to her. He knew without being told that someone had hurt her that evening, and he had the strangest sensation of wanting to savage the person responsible. Strange because the tightness in his chest told him he *was* that person. He was the one who had thrown her life into turmoil. He was the catalyst in her troubled existence. "I'm sorry," he said again, his voice husking. "You have to believe that."

Hot tears rolled down her cheeks.

"Cat," he said softly, "you are tearing me apart. What's wrong?"

Cat's heart fisted painfully. She was so full of anguish she couldn't do anything but shake her head. It was all there, lodged in her throat, the years of heartbreak, the impulse to lash out. She wanted to hurt him. She wanted *him* to hurt the way she did. And yet she knew if she let free all the torment inside her, she would never stop. She would rail and cry and thrash at him until she crumpled into a heap—and she couldn't let that happen. She couldn't break down in front of him. She *hated* him . . .

"I'm sorry," he said again. And then the rushing river swept up his words and whispered them over and over until there was no other sound in the park.

Seconds flashed by as they stood apart from each other. Moonlight washed over them, accentuating the distance between their bodies and the intensity of their discordant needs. Cat was paralyzed with conflict. Blake was held in check by the fiery brilliance of her tears, and by his sudden, lacerating need to touch her.

He held out his hand.

"Cat . . . I'm not going to hurt you."

He watched her chest heave with a sigh, saw her body shudder violently, her head jerk up. And something broke open inside him. He couldn't take it anymore, the gut confusion, the pain. He surged toward her and swept her into his arms.

"No!"

The scream burst from somewhere deep in Cat's spine. She felt the heat of him, the sweet, hard shock of his body, and all she could do was slam her fists against his chest and moan. "No!" she pleaded, flailing at him. *"No—"*

"Cat—it's all right."

His voice was low and savage. He held her so tightly she couldn't breathe, as though he meant to squeeze the agony out of her with the heat and hardness of his arms. Pain flared through her body in a roaring, fiery wave. It burned her like a torch. It left her weak. A sob nearly closed off her throat.

"D—damn you, Wheeler."

She moaned as he loosened his hold and touched her hair, caressing her with a tenderness that was nearly unbearable.

"Let me hold you, Cat," he said, his voice whisper-harsh. "Just for now, baby, until the pain is gone."

Yes . . . she wanted that. It nearly killed Cat as she realized she wanted him to hold her. All of the searing torment inside her seemed to collect and explode in her throat. Struggling free of him, she pushed back and was stunned at what she saw. His face was ravaged with emotion. His eyes were dove gray and piercingly beautiful. They reflected her pain.

"Damn you," she whispered, sobbing.

Tears soaked her contorted face.

Blake's heart twisted at the sight of her. Without a word he gathered her back into his arms, and she collapsed against him with a soft, heartbreaking sound. He felt a convulsion take her. It caught him, too, spasming deep in his center. She stiffened through the shock wave, gasping softly, and then she flowed back against him, as though all the rage were draining out of her. Her face was wet with tears, her body sweet and hot with the fever of her turmoil.

Cat . . . sad, beautiful Cat.

She was fragile in his arms, as breakable as bone china. Lord, he thought, how easy it was to overlook her fragility. She hid it too well under fiery outbursts. She was desperate to protect herself, to hold people off, and she'd almost succeeded. He'd forgotten an essential truth about her. She *was* broken, inside.

She sighed and shook against him. The need to shelter and protect her was satisfying to Blake's soul. At the moment it felt as though it were all he would ever need—her gentle, rhythmic respiration, her soft form molded against him. And yet for all his contentment his body was reminding him in subtle ways that the other needs were there, too. He was aware of a low, insistent pressure in his loins, and a sweet, rising heat in his muscles.

He closed his eyes and cupped her head with his hands, feeling her heartbeat quicken a little. He wanted to stroke her face and dry her tears. He wanted to kiss her sad, lush mouth. Instead, he whispered to her, telling her how beautiful she was and how nothing would ever hurt her again.

Tears burned Cat's eyes as she let herself be gentled and caressed. It was heaven and hell in his arms. It felt like a betrayal of her deepest self, and at the same time it felt as though she belonged there. With him. His arms were warm and strong and sheltering. His body heat flowed over her raw nerves like a balm. A sigh welled inside her, laced with poignancy.

She marveled at his melting gentleness, at his ability to hold her and stroke her, seemingly forever. It was only when he murmured her name and touched her chin with his fingers that she felt a little flutter of fear.

She resisted him at first.

Even as he feathered her jawline, gently, irresistibly.

At last she surrendered to the urgings of his hand, and her breath caught as she let him tilt her face up. Her mind told her what she would see. Silver eyes. A powerful man, sweetly tortured.

"Was it me, Cat?" he asked. His voice roughened with emotion. "Did I hurt you that badly?"

Tears welled in her eyes.

He blotted them with his fingers, gently, and then, finally, irresistibly, he touched his lips to her cheeks, to her damp eyelashes . . . and to her trembling mouth.

Something surged in Cat as he kissed her. A sensation that was as naked and sweet as the river glittering in the moonlight beside them. It was energy in its purest form. Light curled deep within her, soft and sparkling. It fanned upward and outward, filling her until she could feel it everywhere, even beneath her closed eyelids. Yes, she wanted this, his touch, his kiss. She needed this, desperately. Every nerve in her body was singing out its need.

He whispered her name. He touched her throat.

Longing soared inside her. She shook with the suddenness of it. Her body tightened, and almost as swiftly resistance resurged. *Heartbreak.* She knew the price of her needs. She knew what loving him would bring. Certain heartbreak!

Blake sensed her resistance even before she stopped him.

"Blake, please . . . *don't.*"

She caught hold of his hand, an entreaty in her voice. She was asking him not to take advantage of the emotion that was trembling through her limbs. What she didn't know was that her eyes were contradicting her words. They were dizzy with desire, wild with secret yearnings. Her soft desperation was an aphrodisiac. It tore him apart. *It made him hard.*

"I can't do this," she said, "I can't make love with you."

Blake felt the kick in his stomach muscles. He searched her eyes, mesmerized by the little shocks of fear and excitement he saw in their depths. "'We won't then, if that's what you want. *Is* that what you want, Cat?"

"Yes," she said, a whimper in her throat. But at the same time that she said it, she stunned him by reaching up to caress his mouth. Her fingers trembled as she touched him, and Blake's gut spasmed with physical desire. His heart burned with tenderness. She wanted this as much as he did, but she was frightened out of her mind.

He took her into his arms and held her with an urgency that brought him the most exquisite pain he'd ever known. Lord, but she tore him apart. She made his muscles fist and his heart labor. Holding her wasn't enough anymore. His body had other needs. His body was nail-hard.

She moaned softly as he released her and tilted her face up. He caressed her lipline and felt the unsteadiness in her mouth. "Let it happen, Cat," he said. *"Let it happen with me,"*

Cat wet her lips, sighing, torn.

She had never thought of a man's eyes as beautiful, but Blake Wheeler's were. They were suffused with tenderness and lightning-hot with desire. White hot. More than beautiful. *Irresistible.* Even as she allowed herself to relax a little, she could feel the sensations building up inside her again, taking shape. They were as reverberant as church music, as sweet and sharp as the chords of an organ.

His hand was warm against the slender column of her throat. With every flicker of his thumb along her lips, Cat felt a draining urgency. He was telling her what it would be like when he touched her that way everywhere, all over her body, when he saturated her senses with sexual longing.

A moan welled in her throat.

She could feel the rigidity of Blake's fingers as he stroked her face. The gentleness was bleeding out of him as the demands of his body mounted. He was hurting too.

"Cat," he said, "what do you want?"

With a soft moan she ended the immediate torment. Her eyes told him what she wanted. Him. Love. *Heartbreak.*

Nine

Cat reached out to touch him, and Blake captured her hand, dwarfing its delicate bones with the sheer size of his. "Can you feel it, Cat?" he asked, holding her palm to his chest, pressing it into smooth muscle and up against the thrilling jolt of his heart.

Cat gasped softly as he slid her hand over the washboard ridges of his stomach and along the sinewy steel of his thighs. She was so startled she could only nod her head. She felt plenty. He was stunningly hard. Everywhere.

"It's racking me up," he said, bringing her fingertips to his lips. His voice was husky, vibrant and low. "This need I've got for you. It's getting painful, Cat."

Cat's heart was frantic. The instinct to pull away from him flashed through her psyche, but she couldn't. He held her paralyzed with the sensual strokes of his thumbnail along her inner wrist. And then he brought her to him. Curving his hand to the nape of her neck, he reined her in with the finesse of a handler subduing a beautiful, wild animal.

"Racking me up, Cat."

He brushed his forefinger over her lips, then took possession of her mouth, slowly and sensually, with a restraint that made her feel as though she might go crazy if he didn't drag her into his arms and kiss her senseless. His lips tantalized her, sipping and pulling gently, as though she were an ice cream confection meant to be savored rather than devoured. He wasn't acting like a man in need! Or perhaps he didn't understand that she wanted this, too. She wanted *him!*

Passion flared inside her, sharp and irresistible. She moved against him instinctively, arching from the small of her back and enticing him with the buttery softness of her breasts. A kind of sexual recklessness overtook her as she pressed against him, sinking her hipbones into the solid heat of his body. It would have been a potent invitation to most men, but somehow he held back.

Like a demon he feathered her skin lightly, delicately with his lips, and breathed shocking suggestions against her shell-pink earlobes. Unbearably sensual murmurings aroused her cheekbones and temples and eyebrows. Her nerves fluttered painfully and her stomach clenched. It was rapture, shameless and stingingly sweet. He teased her with his mouth until she felt as though she were splitting apart somewhere in the deepest part of her, until she was wet and wilder for sex than she'd ever been in her life.

"Blake, God . . . hold me, ta—"

She broke off as a shudder racked her.

"Take you?" he said. His eyes went silver with desire.

His breathing changed, faster, tighter. He cupped her hips with his hands and brought her up against him, staring into her eyes. The hardness she'd touched a moment before was now pressed against her, *everywhere.* She moaned out a soft, wild sound as he bent toward her. His kisses were fire. They were quick, hot flares of passion. She yielded under him, moaning again as he broke loose and crushed her mouth under his. It was ravishment of the most thrilling kind. It was her fantasy. . . .

Cat was waiting to be taken, violently, sweetly—dragged to the ground and made love to, swept into sexual oblivion. She felt a shudder go through his muscles, and then, oddly, he seemed to regain a measure of control, to curb the stampeding energy inside him.

Blake was torn by his own needs. He was experiencing the driving miracle of raw sexual heat and the heady power that came with controlling it. Seared by the softness of her mouth and body, he was learning that a man could want a woman so badly that it felt like physical torture. Every cell in his body ached for contact, and yet he wanted to make the moment last forever. He wanted to feel as though he were going to die before he took her, and he wanted her to die when he did.

He caught her face in his hands and breathed kisses all over her flushed skin. And then he held her back, taking in the dark riot of her hair and the passion that enflamed her. The sight of her high breasts and long, sleek legs brought him pain as he flashed on the exquisite relief they promised. He imagined her taking him, sheathing him in ecstasy. He imagined her soft coital cries and sighs.

He'd shocked her on the terrace with a sexy proposition. Now those words felt like a promise. "I'm going to lift your skirt, Cat," he said, his stomach clenching. "Sweet, sad Cat. I'm going to take you right here in the park."

Her eyes flashed with desire, but her body flinched as though he'd knocked the breath out of her. "Is that what you want from me?" she questioned softly. "Sex? Is that *all* you want?"

"All I want?" He glimpsed a sparkling of agony in her eyes. "What I want, Cat," he said, "what I really want is to make it better. I want to take you in my arms and burn away the past."

Burn away the past . . .

Blake watched the light show of emotion that animated her features. Fear, desire, heartache. He witnessed the feelings moving through her, shaking her, and marveled at her ability to withstand so much turbulence.

She stared up at him. "Yes . . . I want that too."

Wildly unsteady, she placed her hand on his chest and held it there as though she wanted to reexperience the thundering rhythm of his heart.

His nervous system registered her distress, the trembling hands, the ragged intake of air. He cupped her face and gazed down at her, surging with tenderness. She was wistful, beautiful in her anguish. He stroked her with his fingertips, caressing her downy jawline, her soft, burning mouth. He thought it was fear shaking her body. He was wrong.

"Lift my skirt," she said tremulously. "Make love to me."

She swayed against him, agonizingly wanton, and the shivery swing of her breasts was enough to ruin a saint's resolution. Her skin was silk, her hair a fire storm. The good people of Cameron Bay called him a man with dreams. He sure as hell had a dream now, and it was her. Her, moaning under his hands. Her, hot and sweet beneath his body, wet and yielding, *her.*

He tangled his hands in her hair and kissed her long and hard. Her mouth was a living, burning thing under his. Her body was meltingly urgent. Blake grasped the skirt of her dress, and by the time he had the silky material up to her thighs, he was so hard he was bursting.

Cat moaned as he crushed her dress in his hands and drew it up her body. She wore only panties, a lacy garter belt, and nylons—and as he exposed her buttocks, she felt the cool night air ribbon through her legs. It touched the heat of her inner thighs and sent a painful shock of awareness through her. He meant to make love to her with all of the tenderness and savagery inside him. He meant to drag her to the ground and ravish her just as she'd fantasized.

That realization flooded her body with waves of lush sexual stimulation. Her breasts tightened. Warmth and wetness welled between her legs.

Blake dipped down and swept her into his arms, carrying her to a concealing thicket of shrubbery, lowering her to the ground. Within seconds of their lips touching, they were adrift in soft green grass, gloriously entangled, sweetly frantic. Cat was vaguely aware of clothing being dispensed with, panties, hooks, and zippers, and then all she knew was the torment of his hands as he opened her legs and caressed the silk of her thighs.

She couldn't bear the stimulation, and she cried out with dizzy pleasure as he caught her up in his arms. She felt herself being pulled with him to a sitting position, and then suddenly she was lifted over his legs.

He settled her on his lap, straddling him. It was a position that made Cat instantly vulnerable—and available—to him. The awareness sent sweet shocks of desire through her. Heat rose from the tightening of her muscles. And then he touched her inner thigh and startled a gasp out of her. She convulsed as he caressed her gently, nearing the source of her excitement with every stroke of his fingers.

The need rising inside Cat was riveting beyond anything she'd ever experienced. She was desperate to become part of him. She wanted his body inside hers, seeking, plunging. Recklessly she buried her hands in his hair and grasped urgent handfuls as she strained for that essential connection. His sex touched her, stroked against her opening, and she gave up a choked sound, arching her back.

She ached for the potent force of his body, and he didn't disappoint her. He gripped her by the waist and gently eased her down onto his rigid flesh, shuddering as she tightened with excitement.

She shivered and cried, astonished at the sensations.

"Easy, Cat, easy," Blake rasped, fighting for control. But control was no longer possible. Racked with need, Cat was beyond constraints or caution. Heedless of the consequences, she drew her nails down his back and startled a growl of excitement out of him. He gripped her savagely and drove into her melting softness with a deep and merciless thrust. All the way in. Pleasure rocketed through her, vibrating clear up into her throat.

Tears stung Cat's eyes as a sudden brilliance flared inside her. She couldn't stop crying as his lovemaking shook her body. She didn't fully understand the depth of her emotion at that moment, or even the deeper meaning of the act. As a torch cauterizes wounds, their fiery coupling was sealing the emotional rift within her, a lifetime of warring emotions. Love and hatred were being fused by fire, healed by passion.

But Cat was lost in the rising flurry of her own heartbeats, in the ragged sounds of Blake's breathing. She only knew about the pleasure he was giving her at that moment—sweet, racking pleasure and heartbreaking joy.

Moments later, using his powerful arms and thighs as leverage, Blake pulled her with him, and they rolled to their sides. "I need you underneath me," he said, rising over her, "wrapped around me. I need to see the sweetness, Cat, to hear you whimper while I move inside you."

A sound of ecstasy came from deep within Cat as he reclaimed her, easing deeply into her body and flexing wondrously inside her. She caught hold of his hips as he thrilled her with another glorious stroke. His eyes were lightning, silver with heat and need. Choked cries rocked through her as he impaled himself in her softness again and again, driving deeply and powerfully.

Fragrant grass cushioned their union, and the river below played tumultuous background music.

Cat's entire mind was drawn into the low, bursting life inside her. With every movement, every shiver and shake, her body surged and tightened. She felt the aching cry for release flare through her and knew that what was coming would be the deepest pleasure she would ever have.

Blake groaned in surprise as her muscles quivered and tightened around him. He couldn't catch his breath for a second. And then she began the cries of completion, and her abandon took him over the edge. He shuddered inside her, losing the rhythm of his thrusts, losing his mind. The hard heat in his groin burst into flame, immobilizing him. The blaze was ineffably beautiful, an inferno that threatened to consume him. All he could do against its roaring heat was to hang on to the woman in his arms and absorb her quaking cries.

For a long time afterward, tangled in each other's arms, Cat and Blake were oblivious of everything but their own perfection. Cool air surrounded them like a halo, its chill held back by the heat of their bodies.

Cat's first awareness was of the whispering sounds of the river. Listening to its tranquil murmurs, she curled up in Blake's arms and welcomed the tenderness of his kisses as he brushed her closed eyelids and her forehead with his lips. For the first time in many years she felt at peace inside, as though she'd completed an arduous journey. Her heart was quiet, steeped in the wonder of its own completion.

Beyond the physical pleasure, Blake felt a kind of absolution, as though he'd been temporarily cleansed of the driving ambitions and careless mistakes of the past. He also wondered at the absolute serenity of the woman in his arms. All the tension seemed to have gone out of her. She made him think of a violin string, strung tight for years and suddenly released. She seemed so transformed he wondered if the dark-eyed hellcat was gone forever, the anger spent with her physical passion. Her shiver told him she could still be affected by the elements.

"Maybe we ought to go in search of warmth and shelter," he suggested. "Cameron Bay isn't known for its balmy nights."

"Not yet . . . I don't want to leave this place yet." Her uptilted head revealed the soft curve of her upper lip.

The temptress has an angel's smile, he thought.

Moments later she acquiesced to letting him drape his jacket over her shoulders.

"Did you ever do this in high school?" she asked him, snuggling into the enclosing warmth of his arms. "Did you ever stay out all night?"

"I stayed out all night," he said laughing, "but I never did *this.*"

She laughed, too, and suddenly it was an inside joke. He loved the husky sound of her laughter, and the special intimacy that passion had created between them. He caught hold of her hands and tucked them under his shirt to warm them.

His heart hesitated as she began to draw her nails through his body hair, combing it. He closed his eyes and leaned back against the tree behind him. It was about as sweet a feeling as a man could have, he decided. She placed her hand over his heart, as though measuring the beats, and Blake thought he'd ascended into paradise. Her voice drifted up to him, soft, almost shy.

"Did you know that I loved you once," she said.

Blake hesitated, not sure he'd heard her right. As the words gathered meaning, the heart she was warming with her hand nearly exploded inside him. *"What?"*

He sat up to look at her.

"It's true." She tried to shrug it off. "I was just a kid. You wouldn't remember."

In *love* with him? Blake pressed his hand over hers. "Don't be so sure. I remember the teenage bombshell who walked into my office like it was yesterday."

"Actually"—her voice softened, saddened—"I had

a younger kid in mind, but it wouldn't surprise me if she—if that teenage bombshell—was in love with you, too."

"I think I want to hear about this. *All* about it."

She smiled and sighed, obviously embarrassed. "It was so long ago, Blake. It doesn't matter."

"Hey," he said, "it matters."

Cat wondered if she ought to fill him in on the details of her childhood crush, then decided it couldn't hurt. She'd already let it slip, and he would probably find it amusing.

Blake found it anything but. Her voice was unsteady as she recounted the day he'd come to her house and given her mother the check, and he was immeasurably touched by the story.

She was silent for a while afterward. "I was a weird little kid," she said finally. "You probably didn't know I existed."

She was slumped gracefully against him, and stroking her own arm, but not in any sensual way, more in the manner of a child seeking comfort.

"I knew the D'Angelos had a child," he said, sensing this wasn't going to be the answer she wanted. "But I didn't know she was a tender thirteen-year-old who thought I was descended from Olympus. Things might have been different if I had."

"How?"

She wasn't going to let him bluff his way through this, was she? He could see by her searching expressing that the question was crucial. "Cat, I didn't know you then. I wish I had, but I didn't. Can't we start from here, from now?"

She sat forward, pulling out of the circle of his arm. "No, I don't think so. . . ."

"Why not?"

"There are things we have to talk about—"

"I thought we just burned the past away."

"Not all of it, not my trial." She took a protracted breath, then she looked up at him. "I didn't steal the T-bird."

Blake was aware of a hot prickle of surprise in his jaw as he stared at her. He nodded slowly. It didn't even occur to him to question her. He'd probably always known on some level. He'd certainly suspected it, right up until the moment that she'd become seductive.

"You're a couple of years too late with that information," he said quietly. "Why didn't you tell me?"

She began rubbing her arm again. "Would you have believed me then?"

"No . . . probably not." She was nailing him to the wall. One nail at a time.

"I may have had lousy judgment at sixteen, but I did have a little pride left, even after that fiasco in your office. What was I supposed to do, Blake? Throw myself on your mercy? It would have destroyed every shred of self-respect I had."

In the moments that followed, Blake came face-to-face with the issues he'd rationalized away so many years ago. She was right. He wouldn't have believed her innocent. He had needed her to be guilty. Perhaps to assuage his own guilt for his part in the seductive episode in his office. Or to justify his need to win his first case and rid the streets of "dangerous criminals" like Cat D'Angelo. God, what a hypocrite he was.

Neither of them spoke as the river surged below them. There was a sound of wingbeats in the trees, and Blake remembered absently that a world still existed out there beyond the bubble of their immediate concerns.

"Maybe there's something I can do," he said.

A bittersweetness crept into her voice. "You're a couple years too late."

"But if I could do something, would you want me to?" Something surged in Blake's heart as he thought about announcing her innocence to the citizenry of Cameron Bay. The ultimate atonement. *I wronged this blameless woman, folks.*

A smile twisted his lips as he caught himself. He

wasn't an aspiring politician for nothing. He was wringing every bit of drama out of the situation. The wronged woman, the repentant DA, the storybook love affair. That's it, Wheeler, he thought, go for the glory.

Cat was staring at the river as though she'd come to a decision. "No," she said finally, releasing them both with her sigh. "I made the choice not to testify. It may have been the wrong choice at the time, but it was my decision then, and my responsibility now."

A winsome smile graced her face as she turned to him. "I was a pretty stubborn kid. I don't think you could have changed my mind if you'd—"

She broke off as though she'd heard something, then she jerked up, concerned. "I think there's someone—"

The words lodged in Cat's throat as a beam of light flashed over her, blinding her.

"Police," a male voice barked. "What's going on here?"

Cat's fear of the police was still instinctive. She clutched Blake's coat around her. "Nothing! We were just talking."

"Officer—" Blake pushed to his feet and extended a hand to Cat, helping her up.

The light flashed over Blake, illuminating him from head to toe. "Mr. Wheeler?" the man said. "Is that you?"

Cat got the spotlight treatment next. A cold jolt of reality hit her as she became aware of the sorry condition that she and Blake were in. The officer's imagination must be going wild, she thought. They were both disheveled and half-dressed. She was shoeless and bare-legged. Blake had grass stains all over his shirt.

The light clicked off, and the officer exhaled heavily, apparently burdened by the struggle between duty and discretion. "Listen, Mr. Wheeler," he said, "why don't you take this, uh, young lady home now. You folks could get hurt out here this time of night."

Truer than he knows, Cat thought.

"If anybody asks," Blake told the officer, kneeling to pick up a shoe, "tell them we were mugged."

The man nodded at them and walked away, his expression hidden by the shadows. "Right, sir, I'll do that."

"Where are we going?" Cat sat forward as Blake swung the Corvette off the main drag and headed for the bay area.

"I'm taking you to my place."

"I'd rather not—"

"We've got things to talk about, you said it yourself. At least we won't be interrupted at the cabin."

"You're taking me to the cabin to talk?"

He drove for several seconds before glancing at her. "I don't want this night to be over yet." His gray eyes flickered over her. "Do you?"

Cat turned to the darkness ahead. He knew the answer.

They reached the cabin a short time later, but she didn't wait for him to come around and let her out. She needed control at the moment, even over the little things. The incident with the officer had made her acutely aware of what she and Blake had just done. Passion in a *park*? A *city* park? *With the district attorney?*

She'd spent ten years cleaning up her act, and now, when that bit of news got out—and it would— she knew exactly what the local folks were going to think. They'd say she tempted poor Blake Wheeler, drove the sweet boy right out of his mind.

The hushed conversation between Sam Delahunt and his cronies came back to her, and she glanced at Blake as they walked toward the cabin. He was so handsome in his dishevelment, he made her throat ache. He looked strong, sure, incorruptible. But was he? Was she ruining Blake Wheeler? The irony of that possibility struck her immediately. They'd just made love in a park and she was worried about *his* reputation.

The cabin was spacious and impressively furnished with antiques and overstuffed couches in tweeds and plaids. The accents were nautical, a huge brass barometer and an open captain's log. Set against the far wall, a lighted cabinet held some of loveliest myrtlewood carvings that Cat had ever seen.

Taking it all in, her sense of irony darkened. The Wheeler compound was hallowed ground, native soil of the town's most prominent citizens, home of the future governor, unless Blake decided to go for bigger things and run for sun god. The reasons she shouldn't be there stacked up in her mind, and they were pervasive: emotional, social, professional. Even the Sinclair case could be jeopardized by a personal relationship between them.

"This is crazy," she whispered.

"Yeah, it does feel that way, doesn't it?"

She turned to him. "Why am I here?"

"So we can get to know each other? How does that sound?"

"It sounds crazy." She threw up her arms. "I come from the west side. Tonight was one thing, but we can't be together, Blake, not in any long-term sense."

Blake looked at her steadily, thoroughly, taking in her dishabille and her spirited beauty. He needn't have feared the premature demise of the hellcat. This was one woman who really knew how to create distance when she was threatened. "We can be anything we want, don't you know that?"

Cat couldn't believe what she was hearing. "When did you become a romantic?" Traces of skepticism overrode the unsteadiness in her voice.

"An hour ago in Mariner's Park. I'm a late bloomer, but I have a feeling it's a long-term condition, to use your phrase."

Cat shook her head. It was impossible to hold the line with this man. He didn't play by the rules. He seemed to know what she wanted to hear. And then he said it. Just when she *didn't* want to hear it. She responded with the first thing that came to mind. "What about sex then?"

"What about it?"

"Well . . . it's certainly no basis for a relationship."

"No argument there."

"My point," she said, "is that our relationship—if you can call it that—*is* based on sex. Besides, it's all you ever talk about."

"What?"

"*Sex.*"

He laughed. "You're the one who's been talking it up pretty good so far."

Her sigh said it was hopeless. "See—see there. We can't even have a meaningful conversation. We're incompatible except for . . . heavy breathing."

"And rolling around half-naked in the grass. We're pretty good at that too."

"Blake!"

He surrendered gallantly. "I'll make you a deal. There will be no heavy breathing tonight, or anything else that could be construed as sexual. We'll do something meaningful, if that's what you want." He sat on the couch and patted the cushion next to him. "We'll play a game. Come on over here."

Cat remained where she was. "Why am I sure you don't mean Scrabble."

"Secrets. Ever played it? You tell me a secret— something you've never told anyone—and then I tell you one. It's a great way to get to know someone."

"Undoubtedly."

His eyes turned smoky as he took in her features. "I have this burning desire to brush the tangles out of your hair."

She pointed a finger at him. "You *promised.*"

"That wasn't sexual, D'Angelo, that was my secret. Now let's hear yours."

Ten

"I never permit liberties to be taken with my hair, *Wheeler.*" Cat cocked an eyebrow. "Apparently not all of us have learned the lessons of history. You've heard of Samson? Marie Antoinette?" She tossed him a "so there" smile.

Blake looked thoughtful. "If I remember correctly, it was Marie's head, not her hair—"

"Same principle." Cat sat herself on the arm of the sofa nearest her, and this time she tossed him an imaginary ball.

Blake caught the ball, and her meaning. It was his turn again. "Let's see. I can balance a pencil on my upper lip for seventy-two and a half seconds."

"That's not a secret."

"It is when you hold the city council record, and your toughest opponent is the mayor." He shot her a wink. "Now you—quick. The game works better when you keep it moving."

"Okay, I read palms." Not exactly true, but she had dreamed of being a fortune-teller when she grew up.

"Kid stuff," Blake said, scoffing. "I want to hear about your darkest vices, your demon of demons, the monkey on your back, if you will."

"Cheese puffs."

"Cheese puffs?" Blake's double take became an intrigued smile. He lifted his shoulders. "We were made for each other."

"What? You too?" She laughed out loud. "You're kidding! Do you have any? Here? In this house?"

His eyes shimmered with mischief. "As a matter of fact, I do. Want to negotiate?"

"You're low, Wheeler."

Blake Wheeler *was* low. Nothing could convince him to produce the cheese puffs but Cat's agreement to let him brush the tangles from her hair. And Cat, weak-willed woman that she was, agreed almost immediately. A secret she had neglected to tell him was that having her hair brushed was almost as guilty a pleasure as Ackerman's.

Sunk in the plush cushions of the sofa, she knew at the first touch of his fingers that she was in trouble. The man's hands! *Telepathic.* Finally, sighing at her fate, she let him do what he would with her hopelessly tangled mane of mahogany.

He sat behind her on the sofa back, armed with an antique hairbrush and a breathtakingly light touch. A man of seemingly infinite patience, he eased the worst tangles out, then he gradually increased the pressure until the brush was gliding the full length of her tresses in long, endless strokes.

"You've got good hair," he said, scooping it up from her neck and lifting the silky weight of it in his hands. "A man could die happy with this streaming over his chest."

"Don't start, Wheeler," she warned, her voice grainy.

Cat could hardly believe what was happening to her heart as he worked and sifted through her hair. His ministrations were heaven. His long fingers were melting her neck muscles to warm syrup, and the gentle rake of the horsehair bristles against her scalp was tingly and sensual.

It stimulated nerves in the oddest places, including the inside of her elbows and the slightly ticklish area just below her ribcage. Sometimes she felt the sensations on the surface of her skin, and sometimes they were inside, and slower, like warm fingers caressing her.

Seduction by hairbrush, she thought, closing her eyes. Lord, it was good. How long had it been since a man had brushed her hair? Never, she realized with a start. Not like this. No man had ever cared for her like this.

He set the brush down finally, but he wasn't through with her. Each butterfly touch of his fingers on her temples and nape was wickedly pleasurable. "What are you doing now?" she murmured.

"Just locating your pressure points. Relax."

Relax? She was so limp with pleasure by the time he located the pressure points behind her earlobes that she came dangerously close to suggesting they forget their agreement and go for another roll in the grass.

If Blake saw the desire in her eyes, he didn't act on it.

"You need a bath, D'Angelo," he said, rubbing a smudge from her chin. "I'll run the water."

"We have an agreement—" It was a puny protest.

All he did was smile. "I said I'd run the bath, D'Angelo. Not give you one."

Moments later, Cat was soaking in an antique, claw-footed bathtub full of lilac-scented water. She relaxed with a deep sigh and promised herself that when she had finished the bath—and the cheese puffs—she would go home.

The languid movement of the water was hypnotic, and she was drifting off when a buzzing sound roused her. Blake's voice, low and amused, came through the static. "I've got a special going on back scrubs," he said. "Interested?"

"Where are you?" She scanned the room and spotted an intercom grid next to the medicine cabinet mirror.

The door opened a moment later. "I'm right here," he said, looking casually devastating in pale blue jeans that rode low on his hips. He wore nothing else, no shirt, no shoes. His body hair was still damp from the shower he must have just taken, and burnished gold ringlets clung to the flare of his pectoral muscles and made a dizzying V down his belly. Physically, he was everything she'd ever dreamt of. And much, much more than she could handle.

Staring at him, she realized suddenly why being in his home was so threatening. He'd been a phantom in the park, muted by shadows, a demon lover. Now he was real—warm flesh, hot blood, a man in virile, living color.

"Back scrub time," he said, displaying his hands to her, front and back. "These have been known to bring prayers to the lips of nuns."

Her laughter was soft and despairing. "I can believe that."

Moments later he was lathering her shoulders with slow, circling strokes. "I used to fantasize about this when I was a kid," he said.

"About scrubbing backs?"

"No." He dipped into the water and brought up a palmful, letting it stream down her shoulders. "About being the water in a woman's bath. That way I'd get to touch and taste her everywhere." He bent toward her and pressed his lips to her hair. "I was a horny little kid."

The water in her bath? Cat was instantly and acutely aware of her own body and the way the water caressed her. Everywhere. The sensations against her skin were breathtaking. She sank down protectively and liquid warmth sluiced through her thighs. Eddying rivulets welled in the curve of her belly and crested on the arc of her hipbones. The water touched her in all of the intimate places that a lover would. It was meltingly sensual. Silky ripples kissed her breasts and sent radiating thrills of excitement through her.

"You're shivering," he said. "Are you cold?"

"No," she laughed weakly, "quite the opposite. Do that thing you mentioned, would you?"

"What thing?"

"Touch me, taste me . . . everywhere."

Cat had never been touched so exquisitely.

Blake handled her as though she was breakable, a woman made of the most delicate Dresden. He dried her with fluffy towels and carried her off to his bed where ebony sheets flowed around her in cool spill streams of silk. He murmured to her and caressed her, feathering her eyebrows and the bridge of her nose and her parted lips. He drifted long fingers over her palms, then laced them though her fingers, drawing them up and down, in and out. Slowly, sensually, he stroked the insides of her wrists and elbows until she could hardly breathe for the pleasure.

"Blake . . . if you don't stop soon, there'll be nothing left of me but a warm puddle."

His answer to that was to drop dreamy kisses along the side swells of her breasts. When he found the sensitive spot below her ribcage, and Cat told him she was ticklish there, he blew gently on the area, a slow draught of air that bathed her in warmth and the minty scent of his breath. It felt so light and exquisite, she invented several more ticklish spots. He obliged her, tracing her skin with jets so deliciously sensual, she melted under them like warm caramel.

And finally, when she asked him if he was ever going to make love to her, he shocked her sweetly with his answer.

"Not tonight," he said, drawing her into his arms. "I made you a promise, remember?"

He kissed the fluttery pulse at her temple and gathered her into the warmth of his embrace as though that was all he would ever need. Her, close. Cat was touched, shaken clear through to her heart.

It was almost as though he knew that even though she'd asked for sex, what she really needed was to be cared for.

It rained during the night. Cat awoke once to a fresh spring shower drenching the windowpane and rinsing clean the countryside. It was dawn when Blake woke her next. He smiled down on her, all golden and tousled, still drowsy with sleep. He made her heart ache, he was so beautiful to her eyes. So male and sexy and artlessly arousing.

Moments later they were making slow, poignantly sweet love as the sun broke over the hills and the birds chirped and splashed in mud puddles outside the window.

It was a languorous odyssey, their lovemaking, as dreamy as the mists that hung over the bay. Blake pleasured her as tenderly as he had the night before, then took the time to show her what gave him pleasure. He was a large man in other places than just his hands, and Cat felt a sharp thrill of excitement as he guided her fingers over his muscular contours. When at last he led her to the searing hardness between his legs, she swallowed a gasp.

He shuddered as she took him in her hand.

A short time later, lodged deeply inside her, he exhaled a male groan of pleasure. "I may never move again," he told her. "This is where I want to stay forever."

She softened with a flush of sexual need. "Oh, you have to move . . . a little . . . eventually."

"I do?" He laughed. "How? Like this?"

His body didn't buck, but she felt the muscles of his thighs tighten, felt him stir inside her, deeply, rapturously.

It set her aflame.

She tightened and sighed, gripping his naked hips and sinking her fingertips into his flesh as he took her down the path of fire. Sweet fire. She cried out at the moment of release, tears in her eyes, her feelings so piercingly tender, her heart so crazy with life and love that it frightened her.

Afterward, long afterward, when he left her to find them some sustenance in the kitchen, she went to the window and stared out at the drizzly, sun-misted world. She folded her arms and acknowledged the rainbow arcing over the bay with a smile. It was beautiful enough to nurture dreams in a girl's heart. Dreams of the right man, togetherness, happily ever after.

Her heart wavered. Her smile turned poignant.

Lord, she was coming down with a bad case of hope.

She turned her attention to the birds fluttering in the puddles and waited for the dangerous feelings to leave. The truth was she wanted all those things, happiness, togetherness. With him. *No wonder she was scared.* Some things were too good to be true. Some things were too good even to be imagined.

Beyond that there was the problem of what had happened between them in the last twenty-four hours. The park encounter was too wild and reckless by far. This morning, too sweet. She lost some part of herself when she was with Blake, some vital element of control. She felt and thought things that would have been inconceivable even a week ago.

He set down a tray of rolls and coffee when he came back into the room. "Am I interrupting something?" he asked, coming up behind her and encircling her waist.

She turned in his arms. "Blake, we have to talk about this thing that's happening between us."

"This thing, as you call it, is beautiful."

"Yes, okay, but what are we going to do about it?"

"You're going to stay with me, here."

"Here? What do you mean?"

"The weekend, Cat, just the weekend."

"And then?"

"We'll play it by ear."

She couldn't fathom his calm. She loved it, but

she couldn't fathom it. "But aren't you frightened, Blake? Doesn't this scare you at all?"

His brows knit quizzically. With an unexpected wrench of despair she wondered if maybe he wasn't feeling any of this as deeply as she was. That thought was too distressing to pursue, and she quickly turned to another line of reasoning. "They're going to talk, Blake. The political bigwigs, even the people—your constituency. They're not going to like this at all."

"Let them talk."

Cat shook her head. He didn't seem to understand what they were up against. Finally she realized she would have to tell him what she'd overheard at the fund-raiser. "There's something you need to know. It involves Sam Delahunt."

She recounted the humiliating story with great difficulty, unable to completely curb the bitterness in her voice as she finished. "So, of course, they assumed you'd drop me once you'd—taken me to bed."

Blake's reaction was swift and furious. He left her at the window and cut across the room. "I'll put a stop to that. I'll tell Sam what he can damn well do with his campaign."

There was a phone on the nightstand. He picked it up and began to punch out buttons.

"Blake!"

She talked him out of his anger with some effort, appealing to his lawyerly side, finally persuading him with the irrefutable logic of simple prudence. "There's too much to lose," she explained. "Your political future, *our* credibility in this pretrial hearing with Johnny."

Finally he promised he wouldn't do anything drastic, for everyone's sake. And then he turned the tables on her. It took him the best part of the morning to convince her to stay the rest of the weekend, but when at last Cat agreed, she did it unreservedly. She would go for broke, she decided. She would ride the express train she'd boarded to the end of the track. At least for the weekend.

They turned out to be two of the most wonderful days of Cat's life. She walked with Blake on the rock-studded beach and they waded in the icy Alaskan currents of the bay. They fished for silver salmon and steamed the five-pounder they caught to mouthwatering perfection in a seaweed-lined pit in the sand. And of course, they made mad, passionate love and ate cheese puffs.

Cat D'Angelo was a happy woman. She'd never felt more blissfully starry-eyed and replete with the goodness of life. It wouldn't have taken much to convince her that she was living out a fairy tale: Cinderella and the Prince, or maybe Sleeping Beauty. Whichever fable it was, it was over too quickly. Sunday night came, and she didn't want to go. She was convinced that the magic would be over the minute she left the compound. Over and irretrievable.

Blake was wonderfully reassuring, even about the prospect of dealing with the slings and arrows of Sam Delahunt and his cronies.

"Everything's going to be all right, Cat," he told her, swaying gently with her in his arms. "I won't string Sam Delahunt up by his ankles because you asked me not to. But I promise you this, nobody's going to hurt you—or us. I won't let that happen."

Safe in his arms, Cat absorbed his passionate promises. Oddly though, what resonated in her mind was a flicker of something deeper she'd seen in his expression several times over the last two days. He looked very much like a man reflecting on the quality of his life, perhaps even meditating on his needs. Needs, yes. She wanted to think it was that.

He drove her home, and beyond the low jazz beat coming from the car stereo, it was a silent, reflective ride. Cat found herself wondering about Blake's early years and the peculiar nature of his deprivations. Peculiar because it was odd for her to think of a Wheeler as deprived. Still, there weren't too many other explanations for the driving hunger of the younger Blake Wheeler. He'd been opportunistic, even ruthless. Her training had taught her that both could be symptoms of emotional deprivation. Those who craved glory were often in need of something else. Love? Acceptance?

As he pulled up in front of the Kirkpatricks' place, she wondered if Blake would ever be able to find what he sought outside of his career. She hoped the promises he'd made that night weren't just idle words. She wanted badly to believe that he wouldn't let anything hurt them.

Please, she thought, *let him mean it.*

Blake hadn't even finished his first cup of coffee before Linda paid him a visit Monday morning.

She walked straight to the chair across from his desk, sat, and stared at him for several seconds before she spoke. "In the park, Blake? Really, couldn't you have waited until you got her home?"

Blake exhaled slowly. "How did you hear about it?"

"My esteemed colleagues in the public defender's office." She waved a hand toward his window. "But you could walk out there on the street and ask anyone. It's all over town."

"I guess good news travels fast."

"Sweetie"—she leaned forward, real concern in her eyes—"what are you trying to do? If this is a fling you're having, I hope it's good and flung, because you're in hot water. Daddy's not very happy—"

"And I'm not very happy with Daddy."

Startled into silence, Linda managed, "You're not?"

"I'm not." Taking advantage of her discomfiture, Blake walked around to Linda's chair and pressed a hand to her elbow. She rose to her feet automatically, and it was only as he escorted her to the door that she managed one last question. "What am I supposed to tell him?" she asked. "Daddy, I mean."

"Tell Sam that what interests me about Cat D'Angelo may well be beyond his comprehension. Tell him I'm in love with the woman." He smiled and shut the door on Linda's astonishment.

A shock wave of apprehension hit Blake as he released the doorknob. He blanked for a second, couldn't even remember what he'd said. Then he raked a hand through his hair, aware of the sweat beading on his brow. In love? If that was true, it was probably a first for Blake Wheeler. He wasn't sure he even knew what "in love" meant. As a kid he'd thought of it as some kind of degenerative condition for which he had a built-in resistance. His parents had never shown any signs of succumbing to the malady either. As an adolescent, he'd witnessed the screwball behavior brought on by his friends' crushes and decided life was easier without that kind of brain damage. Especially the life he had planned.

He walked to the window and stared out. He was aware of the crisp cotton collar against his neck and thought about loosening it. He rubbed his chin instead and experienced the friction of his forefingers against his facial skin. He could even feel the hair on his thighs catching against the fabric of his pants. You're alive, his body was telling him. Your heart beats, your blood flows through your veins, and you feel things, man. Surprise, you feel things deeply.

He turned away from the window and scanned his office, searching for signs of the man he knew. All right, he felt things. But love? Love was too deep a concept for a man who hadn't even finished his second cup of coffee. He did know one thing though—the second burning certainty in ten days' time. Now that Cat D'Angelo had walked back into his life, he wasn't letting her walk out. There would probably be hell to pay for that decision, but he would pay it.

• • •

Cat spent her Monday morning waiting for the other shoe to fall. It did. But it wasn't quite the shoe she expected.

Johnny Drescher arrived for his session with a quirky grin on his face. "Did you really make out in the park with Blake Wheeler?" was the first thing out of his mouth.

She threw her head back in despair. "Who told you that?"

"I don't know," he said, falling into the chair opposite her desk. "I guess it's true, huh?"

It took Cat twenty minutes to dig more than an "I don't know" out of Johnny. Finally, in fear of his young life, he admitted that it was all over Bayside High that she and Blake had been caught in flagrante delicto in Mariner's Park. "And that's not all," he added, a wiseacre grin on his face. "They're saying Wheeler's gone squirrely."

"Squirrely?"

"Yeah, a student intern in the mayor's office overheard Linda Delahunt telling her father that Wheeler's wigged out. I guess he told Linda he was in love with you or something."

Cat was dumbfounded. She cut short the meeting with Johnny, and once he'd gone, she sat in her office with an amazed and utterly stupid grin on her face. In love with her? *Love?* The L-O-V-E kind? The idea was staggering.

Curiosity short-circuited Cat's common sense. She called Blake's office and was told he was in a staff meeting. When Cat left her name, the secretary surprised her with the news that Mr. Wheeler was planning to pick Cat up at six that evening. "I was just about to call you and let you know," she explained.

"Pick me up? For what?" Cat asked.

"Well, I don't know, dear," the secretary said, slightly flustered. "For a date, I suppose."

A date? Cat replaced the receiver, and the silly grin returned. Nervy of him, she thought. Damned nervy, but still she couldn't wipe the smile from her face.

As the day wore on, Cat began to adjust to the idea that she and Blake were an item, mainly because everyone she encountered told her so, including Gwen.

"Apparently you're over your grudge against Blake," Gwen said, a lilt of disapproval in her voice as she hovered in Cat's doorway. "When I suggested you put the past behind you and get on with your life, I wasn't thinking of anything quite so demonstrative, Cat. Certainly not *splendor* in the grass."

Cat felt like a thirteen-year-old justifying an outrageous prank to mom. "Neither was I, Gwen. It just happened."

When Blake showed up at the center with a bouquet of violets that evening, a crowd assembled. Therapists and their clients materialized out of offices, and even the normally discreet receptionist couldn't get her mouth closed.

Most of the neighbors were kibitzing from their porch swings as she and Blake rolled away from the building in his Corvette.

"We ought to set up bleachers," Cat said, waving to Bumper, who was crouched on the sidewalk, playing a fierce game of marbles with his friend Biff.

"And charge admission," Blake agreed.

Cat laughed and swung her head toward Blake. Their eyes connected for a minute, and as the laughter faded, another awareness took over. It was heart-catching and sudden, a glimpse of some emotion that cut right to the core. Cat felt as though the breath had been knocked out of her, but there was only one thought on her mind—Johnny's announcement that morning. *He told Linda he was in love with you. . . .*

Blake broke their connection first. He looked away, aware of the blood pounding through his temples. The sound was like a muted volley of gunfire. He loosened the knot on his tie and heard his own words echoing distantly. *Tell Sam I'm in love with the woman.*

He reached over, flicked on the radio, and the car was filled with the mellow voice of James Taylor singing "Handy Man."

"Nice song," Cat said, suddenly very interested in what might have been a water stain on the lapel of her blouse.

"Right, I always liked his . . . stuff."

After a couple more equally unproductive attempts at small talk, they made the remainder of the trip to Blake's cabin in silence. Cat sat with the violets in her hand, trying to ignore the bouquet, and what it might mean. Blake drove with the concentration of an ambulance driver, never taking his eyes off the road. It was as though neither of them knew quite how to address the emotional static that was spiking the air around them.

Blake made a couple of references to the weather, and Cat had the oddest thought. He seemed almost shy. A smile warmed her lips. Never happen, she decided. Blake Wheeler could walk down Main Street naked and not be self-conscious. The violets were beautiful though, she realized, bringing them to her nose to smell them.

She'd always loved shy men.

Blake seemed to have recovered a measure of his composure by the time they reached the cabin.

"Do you want a drink?" he asked, pouring himself a highball glass nearly full of straight Scotch.

"Yes, please. Some white wine if you have it."

As he turned to her with the wine Cat took a deep breath and released it, along with the question that had been driving her wild with curiosity. "In *love* with me? Blake, did you really say such a thing?"

He left her drink on the bar and took a deep swallow from his own glass. "Who told you?"

That sounded like an affirmation, and Cat could hardly believe her ears. Or her eyes. She watched him pull off his tie and yank open the top buttons on his shirt. She'd never seen him so uneasy. They were right. He *was* squirrely. "It doesn't matter who told me," she said softly. "What's happening to you?"

"Why the hell is everybody asking me that?"

"Because of the way you're behaving." She held up the violets. "Because of these. You're not yourself."

"Right, so maybe I am in love—" He broke off, a glint of trapped frustration in his eyes. Palming the glass of Scotch in his hand, he looked as though he intended to finish the rest of it off in one swallow. And then start in on the bottle.

A flash of silver eyes. "Is that a problem?"

Problem? She was thrilled out of her head. She was also scared half to death at the prospect. "No, not a problem exactly. I just can't quite fathom the idea."

"Neither can I." He stared at her for a long moment, his expression charged with mounting fascination. An ironic smile shimmered as he set down his drink. "I'm willing to work on it though, if you are."

He walked toward her, and Cat could hardly hear herself think over the explosion of excitement inside her. "You know me," she said, breathless, "always the hard worker."

Their first undertaking was a taut, tender kiss. It was the sweetest kiss of Cat's life. She shuddered in his arms, anticipating his low groan of desire. They were well on their way to a soul-scorcher when the phone rang.

Blake broke away with a touch of his lips to her nose and went to pick it up. He listened a minute and handed the receiver to her. "It's for you—Gwen."

Cat answered with the dizzy smile that was becoming her trademark. "Hi, Gwen—what's up?"

"Bad news, Cat. Very bad, I'm afraid."

Cat gripped the mouthpiece of the phone. "What is it?"

"It's Johnny," Gwen said. "The police picked him up an hour ago. He's being held down at the city jail."

Eleven

Blake dropped Cat off in front of the station house, a two-story brick structure with holding cells for juvenile as well as adult offenders. He caught Cat's arm as she pushed out of the small car. "If they give you any trouble about seeing Johnny, tell them I'm on my way. I'll park the car and stop at the desk to find out what they're holding him on."

Because of Cat's counselor-client relationship with Johnny, she was able to see him without any difficulty. She sat in a booth in the visitors' area, waiting for him to appear on the other side of the crosshatched glass. When he did, he looked so pale and frightened that Cat felt sick at heart. She recognized the fear. It was the familiar stench of buildings like this one. It had never left her nostrils, not completely.

"Are you all right?" she mouthed through the glass.

He nodded his head, and Cat tried to smile, but by then she was caught up in the burgeoning memories of her own experience. Chalky blue uniforms, handcuffed wrists, and grimy glass barriers. It was too real, too close to her own nightmare. She could even remember the musty holding tank, the bars, the suffocating claustrophobia.

She had to consciously order herself to pick up

the phone receiver. Once she'd managed it, she signaled Johnny to do the same. "What happened?" she asked him.

"I don't know," he said. "I was walking home from the garbage dump, and the police picked me up."

"What are they holding you for?"

"I don't know—breaking and entering, I think."

Keep asking questions, she told herself. "Breaking and entering what?"

"Somebody's house—" He lifted his shoulders helplessly, and Cat could see he was near tears.

"That's okay," she said quickly, "Blake will find out. What were you doing at the garbage dump?"

"I had my slingshot is all. I was hunting rats. I do that sometimes when my mom works late."

"Does your mother know about this?"

His jaw contracted, fighting emotion. "No—I only had one call. I tried to get you at the center, but you weren't there."

"Don't worry about it," she reassured him. "I'll let your mom know."

With a savage gesture he knuckled the moisture from his eyes. "I don't know what they got me in here for, but whatever they're saying I did, it's a lie." His voice cracked. "I didn't do it, Cat."

"I know you didn't." She swallowed against the sting of tears in her throat. "I'll get you out of here, I promise."

Blake appeared as she was reassuring Johnny and telling him not to worry. With one last attempt at encouragement Cat reminded Johnny that she'd been through it, too, and survived. But her heart sank as she saw the somber look on Blake's face.

She held the phone against her chest. "What is it?" she asked. "Breaking and entering?"

"Yes," he said, "but it gets worse. He's also being held on counts of illegal entry, vandalism, and robbery."

"Oh, God—"

"It was two houses down from the Kirkpatricks' place."

"The place where I'm staying?" Her next words were a faint attempt to assimilate the information. "Someone robbed the Kirkpatricks' neighbors?"

"Not someone, Johnny. Or at least that's what they're saying." He took the phone from her hand. "Let me talk to him."

Cat listened anxiously as Blake probed Johnny for more information. Blake's approach was cautious, almost gentle, but Cat's stomach was tied up in knots long before Johnny had finished his story. The real horror came when she realized that he had no alibi for the time of the robbery. None whatsoever.

Panic hit her. It was the sound of a needle being dragged across a phonograph record. Her thoughts spun back in time, dragging the needle across the surface of her life. She'd had no alibi either. There was no one who could corroborate that she'd been home alone when Cheryl drove up in the car and persuaded her to go for a ride. When the police detective had questioned Cat afterward, Cat had been cooperative. She'd told him everything he wanted to know. Later, much of what she'd said in that session had been used against her.

"Johnny, stop!" she said. "Don't say any more."

Blake frowned at her. "What's wrong with you?"

"You're the DA." Her voice was soft, almost shrill. "You could end up prosecuting him."

"Cat, he's my witness. I'm trying to get to the bottom of this. Maybe we can get him released tonight."

"No!" She pulled the phone from Blake's hand and spoke to Johnny. "Don't say another word! Not until I find you an attorney."

Blake let Cat into the Corvette, slammed her door, and went around to his side of the car. "What the hell was that all about?" he asked, hitting the gas pedal as he twisted the ignition key.

Cat's voice sharpened over the roar of the car's engine. "Johnny has two priors. They're not going to do a kid like that any favors, and you know it." She finished her argument once they'd pulled out of the tiered parking area. "He has to be protected, Blake. Even if you don't prosecute him personally, your office will. He needs an attorney."

"For God's sake, Cat, I wasn't building a case against him. I wanted to hear his side of it."

Blake went silent, negotiating the evening traffic as he made a lane change. Cat swayed and caught her balance against the console, her fingernails creasing the leather. Neither of them spoke for several moments.

"What have they got on him?" she asked as Blake turned down the street that led to the Kirkpatricks' place.

"It's bad," Blake said. "There's an eyewitness. A young girl saw a teenager matching Johnny's description enter the house."

"She saw him breaking in?"

"She said he entered by the front door. At first she thought he lived there, but he was acting oddly enough to make her suspicious."

"Who was this girl? West End?"

"No, she was bicycling through the neighborhood on her way to a friend's."

A bystander, Cat thought, some anonymous bystander who didn't even know Johnny. Frustration sparked inside her, and for one hot, razor-quick second she wanted to cry. Her fingers bit into soft leather, and then, in the rebounding seconds, she caught herself. She was identifying too closely with Johnny's situation, and that kind of self-indulgence was dangerous now. She needed to stay rational, ask questions. It was the only way she could help him.

"What was supposed to have been stolen? Did they find anything on Johnny?"

"Jewelry—rings, watches, credit cards, that sort of thing. Johnny was clean when they picked him up, but he would have had plenty of time to hide the stuff."

Cat's jaw stung as though she'd bitten into sour fruit. The taste filled her mouth as she stared at Blake, and she couldn't swallow it away. "You think he did it, don't you?"

"I didn't say that."

"But you do."

She jerked back as Blake reached for her hand. "What about the Sinclair trial?" she asked sharply. "What happens now?"

Blake downshifted and shot her a glance. "It depends on what happens to Johnny. Without his testimony we haven't got a case against Skip Sinclair. Even with it, Johnny may have been so badly discredited by this that he won't be an effective witness." The car jolted and bounced as Blake drove over the railroad tracks. "Without any new evidence my office will probably have to drop the case."

Cat's thoughts whirred frantically, grabbing at possibilities. "Maybe it wasn't Johnny. Eyewitness testimony isn't infallible. People get picked up by mistake all the time. That girl? How can she be sure *who* she saw?"

Blake's voice took on a firm, calming tone. "The report indicated a positive ID. At any rate, there'll be a lineup. She'll have to pick him out of several other men who match the description."

Another possibility churned into Cat's head. It was crazy, but she said it anyway. "What if he was framed?"

"Framed? Why?"

"I don't know. Maybe someone is setting him up to get the Sinclair case dismissed."

Blake heaved a sigh. "Cat, stop this. You're desperate. You're grabbing at straws."

"Yes, I am desperate! Why aren't you? He's *your* witness. Or maybe you want the case against Sinclair dismissed too? I'm sure it would be less messy that way."

Tears welled in her eyes. She was lashing out, trying to hurt him, and she could see by his expression that she had already done some damage, but she couldn't stop herself. "Prosecuting Skip can't be good for the ol' political career, am I right?"

Blake braked to an abrupt stop. Silently he watched a car pass through the intersection in front of them before he started up again. "So now it's *my* motives that are in question? Next you'll be accusing me of setting Johnny up."

Cat knew an apology was in order, but she couldn't bring herself to make it. She'd only begun to allow herself to trust Blake in the last few days. For most of her life he'd been the enemy. That was the position she knew and understood. That was the battleground she'd fought on. Now that battleground felt more real than the weekend's passion and tenderness.

They arrived at the Kirkpatricks' in silence.

"Do you want me to come in?" he asked.

"No, I don't think so."

She let herself out silently, and Blake made no attempt to stop her until she turned to close the car door.

"I'm on your side, Cat," he said. "And Johnny's. Even if he weren't my witness, I wouldn't want to see anything happen to him. He's a nice kid with a bad hand of cards."

He let himself out of the car on his side and studied her over the low-slung top of the Corvette. "You're the one who's got me scared. If Johnny is guilty—and he could be—you're going to crumble, Cat. I can see it coming already."

"Johnny's *not* guilty—" She pulled back, trying to get control, but her voice broke. "He cried in there, Blake. He cried, and he asked me to help him. He's never done that before."

"Cat . . . maybe you ought to back off a little. You know, let one of the other counselors take over for you."

A premonition flashed in Cat's mind. Her voice dropped low and soft with shock, and she stepped back from the car. "Don't try to have me taken off this case, Blake. I warn you. Don't try to do that!"

She stared at the concern in his handsome features, but all she could see was power. The power of his position, the power to do both Johnny and her harm. With a quick flick of her hand she slammed the car door shut.

Moments later, from the window of the Kirkpatricks', she watched him drive away. She was dry-eyed, but the muted sound inside her head was the shriek of a needle being dragged across a record.

"You didn't see or hear anything unusual that afternoon? You're sure?" Cat peered through the rusty screen door and smiled wearily at the frazzled young mother, who was shaking her head. One toddler in a "Ninja Turtle" T-shirt clung to the woman's leg, and if the noise inside the house was any indication, there were several more little Ninja Turtles inside, all determined to karate-chop the stuffing out of each other.

A child's wail rattled the screen. "I'm real sorry," the woman said. "I have to go now."

Back out on the sidewalk Cat looked up and down the street and wondered if she had the strength to cover the remaining houses. Over the last week she'd scoured not only the Kirkpatricks' block but the adjoining neighborhoods as well, talking to the victims and anyone else who would give her a moment. She finally found two elderly sisters who thought they'd seen the robber, but their account brought her more despair. Their description fit Johnny down to his leather jacket.

All in all it was a week of indescribable torment for Cat. Her feelings toward Blake were so tangled and confused, she avoided his calls for the most part. When she couldn't avoid him, she was vague and noncommittal about their personal situation, and ready with excuses when he asked to see her. He didn't press, much to her relief. He seemed to understand her need for distance.

As the evidence mounted against Johnny, Cat's visits to the boy, and her repeated attempts to encourage him, became increasingly painful. Her reassurances sounded hollow even to her own ears. She had learned through Gwen that Blake had assigned one of the younger DAs to the case. Even that piece of information dragged Cat back into own her personal nightmare. The young ones were aggressive and hungry. They wanted to win. As Blake had wanted to win.

When she learned that the Sinclair hearing had been postponed so the prosecutor's office could "reevaluate" the evidence, she began refusing Blake's calls altogether. She'd seen it coming. There would be delay after delay in the Sinclair case until the whole matter was conveniently set aside. She didn't hold Blake responsible, but she knew that he would ultimately benefit from the Sinclairs' gratitude, and that made her resent his privileged situation all the more.

Every time her phone rang at home or in the office, her turmoil mounted. The price of refusing Blake's calls was losing him, she knew that. He wasn't a patient man by nature, and she couldn't be certain of the strength of his feelings for her. Lord, how many times had she wished she'd never heard of Blake Wheeler. And yet in all her confusion one thing was painfully clear. She cared about him more than she would ever have believed possible. Sometimes she couldn't even breathe right for the misery squeezing her heart. Flashbacks of their weekend flared through her thoughts. She could still feel his hands on her body, in her hair. His passion and tenderness had seared her with their indelible imprint. Yes, she cared. *It would kill her to lose him now.*

She was leaving her house early Friday morning to visit Johnny before going to the center when she noticed the Corvette idling across the street.

Her Mustang was parked in the driveway. She walked toward it briskly, hesitating only as Blake cut the engine and emerged from his car. He slammed the door behind him and stared at her. There was strength in his silence, certainty in his gait, as he began walking toward her.

Cat registered every step he took with mounting alarm. He moved with the swift, singular grace of a man who wanted something, and she sensed that it wasn't going to be easy to refuse him, no matter what it was.

The silence deepened as he approached and stood before her. Neither of them spoke. The emotions connecting them at that moment were too strong for words. And the situation separating them was too painful to be acknowledged.

Silver motes shimmered in his gaze. With no overture other than the hypnotic pull of his eyes, he drew the back of his fingers along her jawline and traced them down her throat. His skin was smooth, but his fingernails rode her flesh. With one stroke she felt both abraded and caressed. Her stomach clenched at the unexpected sharpness of it.

He lifted her face and stroked his thumb across her lips with such lightness she thought for a second that she was going to lose consciousness. She tried to break away, but he said her name, and the sound of it pierced her softly.

Her eyes drifted closed as he bent to kiss her. She arched expectantly, her senses soaring as he hovered over her, his breath hot against her lips. She heard her name again, just before she tasted the heat and honey of his mouth.

Longing flared inside her as he gathered her up in his arms. The kiss was searingly sharp and laced with a bittersweetness that threatened to engulf her. With one touch, one ardent kiss, she was on the brink of no return, ready to make love with him, ready to do whatever he wanted. I can't, she thought, pulling back. I can't, *not this time.*

"No, Blake," she whispered, trying to recover her voice. "This isn't going to solve anything. We're on opposite sides." Her heart spasmed in protest. She wanted him so badly, she couldn't even come up with a believable argument.

"We're not on opposite sides by choice." He caught her by the shoulders and tugged her back to him, dropping a kiss in her hair. "Listen to me, Cat. We each have a job to do. Why can't we do it? Why does this case have to drag us apart?"

He didn't really understand? She struggled free of him, astonished. "Because Johnny's in the middle. Because his freedom is at stake, his whole life."

His hand settled into the curve between her throat and collarbone. "Cat, you have to give up this crusade for Johnny. I wasn't going to tell you yet," he said, "but maybe it's better you hear it now, from me. We have several witnesses. Eyewitnesses. They all saw Johnny go into the house. The case against him is as good as made."

Her throat tightened. "I don't care what anyone saw."

"All the evidence—"

"I don't care about evidence. I care about what I believe, here, in my heart. And what *you* believe. Do you think Johnny did it?"

He stared at her for a long time. "What am I supposed to believe, Cat?"

A moan welled inside her. "You're supposed to believe in what's right, in justice!"

"That's why I can't ignore the evidence."

"Of course not," she said, furious, aching inside. "And that's the fundamental difference between you and me. You believe in evidence, not people. I know Johnny didn't do it. I believe what my heart and my guts tell me."

"Cat, I'm a lawyer. I can't go into a courtroom on gut instinct."

Staring up at him, Cat felt as though she were coming apart inside, ripping like old fabric, and the pain of it was almost familiar now. She had felt it before, with him. Only now she could hear what the torment was telling her. *She couldn't be with him. It would never work.* She would have saved herself so much grief if she'd only listened to her intuition about him before. She had adored him as a young girl. Years later, during the trial, that emotion had gotten twisted up inside her, twisted into hatred. The experience had been shattering. She couldn't go through it again.

"This is a mistake, Blake."

"What is?"

"This, us—you and I. It's not the town or our backgrounds. It's something deeper, Blake. We think differently. We live and breathe differently. It won't work, it *can't*." She could barely get the rest of it out. "And I'm so afraid I'll end up hating you again."

"Cat, don't do this—"

"I have to." She turned away from him and opened the door of her car, wondering if he was going to say something, or touch her. When he didn't, something went numb inside her. Her silent heart refused to respond to the shattering sense of loss, and yet she felt as though she were staring into a light bright enough to burn her eyes. Please, God, let it be over, she thought. Don't let me love him ever again. *But don't let me hate him.*

A moment later, without ever once looking back at him, she pulled the Mustang out of the driveway and drove off into the overcast morning.

Twelve

Blake stood poised on the boat dock in his swim trunks, moonlight washing his body. Bottle-green phosphorescence sheened the glassy surface of the water below him. In the distance, a fish leaped, a scythe of brilliant silver as it slipped back into the reaches of the sound. The only other movement was the smooth slice of his body as he dove into the black mirror that was Cameron Bay.

The pressure hit him first, hundreds of gallons of icy water streaming against his bulletlike form. Seconds flashed by before he felt the freezing temperature bite into his flesh. He continued his descent until his muscles were nearly paralyzed by the cold, then he arced up and shot for the surface, bursting through the transparent glitter, as agile as the leaping fish. It took him several powerful strokes to reach the dock again.

The onshore winds hit him with the chill factor of a winter blizzard as he heaved himself up the ladder and stood on the dock, water streaming down his torso. The cold was punishing, but it was also an anesthetic. It burned the alien feelings from his gut and forced his attention to the icy spasms that gripped his body. With a supreme force of will he brought the concussions under control, one by one, until the only sensation remaining was numbness.

Nothing, he thought, closing his eyes. That was exactly what he wanted to feel. *Nothing.* Sweet oblivion at any price. Even if it took self-inflicted pain to hold off the darkness.

The laughter he exhaled was harsh. Blake Wheeler, the nonbeliever, was being tested. He'd never put any stock in the power of love, or the other intangibles that some people subscribed to. Given his temperament, they too often looked like excuses for irrational behavior, or crutches to prop up a deficit of confidence. But in the last few hours since Cat had told him she didn't want to see him, he felt as though a hole had been seared right through the center of his heart.

He turned back to the dark mirror and watched his image glide over its frozen surface. The moonlight at his back made a giant out of him, a godlike Titan. The irony of it wasn't wasted on him. He'd never been more in the grip of his own puny humanness. Was this the power? Was this what love felt like? A pain that bled the body of every other desire except to extinguish it?

A sound breathed out of him, cold and lonely. No wonder men and women alike quaked in its presence. It was a fearful thing, love. He'd never known it could tear you apart and leave you naked for the wolves.

She knew, though. That was the sadness in her smile. She knew about being torn apart and left naked. About human wolves. The pain seared through him again, and it made him wonder how she'd survived it at sixteen. The kind of hell she'd been through would probably be unfathomable to most people. Certainly to him, until now.

You believe in evidence, not people.

He stooped to pick up the towel he'd dropped earlier and watched his streaming shadow disappear. Was she right about him? He'd stood up for what he believed in once, and the town had made a hero out of him. He'd been full of ideals then, fired up with passion, but something had gone wrong. Maybe glory fed the soul better than self-sacrifice. Somewhere along the line, his dreams of shared progress had turned into the single-minded pursuit of winning legal contests and popularity polls. Hell, he liked being a hero. He'd just forgotten what it meant.

He draped the towel over his shoulders and rose, a decision working in his mind. There were ways to get her back if that's what he wanted. He could put the Sinclair case back on the court docket, then bring in Johnny as a witness. It wouldn't help Johnny's situation, but it might convince Cat that he, Blake Wheeler, had human blood in his veins. The potential risks were enormous. It could mean going up against Delahunt and the power brokers. In that case, Blake's political future would be at stake, maybe even his career as DA.

Her face came to mind then, the fire-tipped hair and flashing eyes, the quiver in her mouth. Her past made her what she was: wounded child, firebrand woman, passionate in her attitudes, torn by her loyalties. She was wired up differently from most people. She still believed in right and wrong. She thought things could be solved by taking the "right" action. Could they? Did anyone else in the world but her believe that?

The pain seared his chest again.

There were ways to get her back, if that's what he wanted.

The setting sun dripped gold through the treetops, liquid warmth that ran down the branches and leaves of the dense forest foliage like teardrops. Cat snapped a branch from a bramble rosebush and brought its delicate pink petals to her nose as she continued her sojourn alongside the railroad tracks. The rose's fragrance sharpened the poignancy she felt. Her freedom to walk in the woods and pick flowers seemed like an undeserved privilege with Johnny still behind bars. Tomorrow he would be formally charged on felony counts of illegal entry, vandalism, and robbery.

She hadn't been able to keep her promise to him. She couldn't free him from jail. She couldn't even tell him when he might be free again. It wasn't that she'd given up. She just didn't know what to do next, or whom to turn to for help. Gwen was busy with her clients and administrative duties and couldn't offer much more than moral support. Blake hadn't attempted to call or contact her since their encounter the week before. Not that she expected him to. She pulled a petal off the rose and let it fall. Or maybe in her heart, she had.

The sky was turning purple and gold by the time Cat reached the Kirkpatricks' place. As she approached the house, she saw Bumper sitting on the front stoop, his collection of marbles spilled out on the sidewalk in front of him.

"Bumper, where have you been?" she called to him. "I haven't seen you all week."

"Been at my gramma's," he said, smiling wistfully. "Wanna play potsies. I'm getting real good."

"Oh, Bumper, I'll bet you are." She knelt to look over his impressive array of cat's-eyes, Black Beauties, and Bass Alleys. He even had a ball bearing in the bunch. The last thing she wanted to do at the moment was play marbles, but Bumper's huge blue eyes tugged at her.

"Potsies it is." She grabbed a stick to mark a crude circle on the cement.

Bumper loaned her a handful of marbles, and they hunkered down for some serious shooting. It soon became apparent that Cat was off her game. Bumper, on the other hand, was every bit as "good" as he'd promised, a five-year-old marble prodigy in the making.

"You got the touch?" Bumper asked hopefully as Cat missed her fourth shot in a row.

"I guess not, Bumper. Not tonight anyway."

"We don't hafta play."

Let off the hook by a five-year-old, she thought. I must be in sad shape. "Maybe I just need a better marble." She picked his prize agate shooter, rolled its sleek heaviness around in her palm, then tucked it into the crook of her forefinger. That was when she noticed the deep crack in the marble. "What happened to your aggie, Bumper?"

He shrugged. "A car runned over it."

"A car? At your grandma's?"

"Nope, in the alley behind my house. Funny car," he said, wrinkling up his nose. "It had a tail like an am—aminal."

"Tail?" The word struck a chord in Cat's memory. She frowned and pressed a hand to her mouth, thinking. The image that came to mind was of Johnny's forlorn figure on the road and a car full of rowdy teenagers roaring up behind him. "Bumper, was the car black? Did it have an antenna like a whip and a raccoon tail?"

Bumper smiled and nodded quickly. "Yeah, neat, huh? Did you see it too?"

Cat didn't answer. She hadn't even heard his last question. She was totally preoccupied with trying to make some sense out of what he'd just told her. "When did you see this car, Bumper?"

"The day my gramma and grampa came to pick me up. I was playing eye-drop out in back."

With a little more probing, Cat put together that Bumper had been practicing marbles in his garage when the aggie had rolled into the alley and the black car had driven by, cracking it.

Cat's head filled with questions. What would that car have been doing in the alley behind Bumper's house? Bumper lived a couple doors down and across the alley from the robbery victims. Cat had talked to his mother once, but she'd said she hadn't seen anything. "What day did your grandparents come, Bumper? Was it last week? On Monday?"

With considerable probing of Bumper's recall, Cat finally narrowed the date down to the afternoon of the robbery. A zing of adrenaline fueled her as she began to realize she was on to something. She hoped Bumper had his information straight! "Who was in the car? Did you see the driver?"

He described two boys, one with the build and ruddy coloring of Skip Sinclair, and a smaller boy, who sounded very much like Johnny by his physical appearance.

"He had on one of those—y'know—leather jackets and red head things," Bumper offered, then added thoughtfully, "kinda like Johnny's."

"A red bandanna? Tied around his head?" Cat's heart was roaring by this time. She sat on the ground, not quite able to deal with what she was thinking. "Did they stop? Did they get out of the car?" she asked softly, almost afraid to hear the answer.

When Bumper nodded, she began to pepper him with questions. Within moments she'd learned enough to know that her instincts of a week ago could well have been correct. Then she'd suspected Johnny Drescher had been set up. Now she was almost sure of it.

"Bumper, would you know those two boys if you saw them?"

He thought about it. "The guy with the leather jacket smiled funny—and he was missing a toof." Bumper opened his mouth wide, stretching his lower lip across his gums as he wiggled one of his baby teeth. "Me too, see? This one's loose!"

Cat pressed her hands to her face and nearly cried. Dear God, she thought, this little boy had seen it happen—the robbers, and the robbery. She caught him gently by the shoulders, choking back the emotion in her throat.

"Bumper," she said, "I need you to come with me, okay? And bring your aggie."

Twenty minutes later Cat pulled her Mustang onto the private road that led to Blake's cabin. She saw the lights on and breathed a sigh of relief. He was home.

She could hardly walk she was trembling so hard. Bumper struggled to keep up with her, and finally she picked him up and carried him, laboring up the steps of the cabin. She found Blake in the kitchen, cooking a steak. He turned as she entered.

She set Bumper down and stood with him beside her, clutching his small hand. "Johnny didn't do it," she said. "I have proof." As she held up the cracked marble, tears began to stream down her cheeks.

Blake stared at her hard—at the beautiful, anguished woman and the bewildered little boy beside her. Emotion hit him like an uppercut. The flesh above his jawbone sucked in and out as he tried to control it. Johnny didn't do it, and her proof was a marble? He didn't know what the hell she was talking about, but it was the best news he'd heard in a week. "Thank God," he said, feeling as though he wanted to cry himself.

It was fortunate that Cat spotted Johnny before he saw her, because the emotion that welled up inside of her at the first glimpse of him nearly undid her. *If ever there was a sight for sore eyes*, she thought as a uniformed matron escorted the teenager into the station house proper.

Dressed in his street clothes—the leather jacket and trademark red bandanna—he looked so grungy and wonderful, so unmistakably Johnny, that Cat could hardly contain herself. She wanted to rush up and hug him, but she knew better. He would be embarrassed beyond belief.

"Johnny?" Cat stepped forward as the boy swung around and saw her. He was still pale and a little shaken, but his eyes lit up and a grin wavered.

"Hi," he said.

He swallowed with some effort, and Cat realized he was struggling with his feelings too.

"He's free to go," the matron said, urging Johnny forward.

Cat took a quick, steadying breath, then she dealt with the awkward moment by linking her arm in Johnny's and whisking him with her toward the door. "Let's get out of this dump," she said.

Sunlight burst over them as they pushed through the swinging doors of the station. It was a breathtaking day, and Cat simply couldn't help herself. A soft sigh of delight escaped her as she breathed in fresh-cut grass, sunshine, and hope.

"Oh, Johnny, don't you just love spring?"

Johnny cocked an eyebrow and extricated his arm from hers with a pained grin. "You're weird," he said.

She nodded, laughing with him. "Weird" wasn't the word for it. She was thrilled about Johnny's release, and at the same time, so muddled about her feelings for Blake that she couldn't get herself grounded. She felt like a plane, circling the clouds and unable to get her landing gear down.

"It looks like Skip's going to do some time," she told Johnny as they stood on the sidewalk in front of the station.

"Bozo deserves it," Johnny muttered.

Cat watched him tug at his bandanna and wondered what was wrong with him. Suddenly he looked up at her and his jaw knotted up painfully. "I just—" He ducked his head, stammering, reddening. "I just wanted to thank you," he finally managed.

The gesture was so wrenchingly difficult for him that Cat fought back another urge to give him a hug. She knew if she did, they might both tear up. "That's okay, Johnny," she said softly. "It was my privilege."

She pressed her tongue up against the back of her teeth, stemming the poignancy she felt. This was a rare occurrence for him, she suspected. He probably hadn't been given too many second chances—or opportunities to thank people for helping him.

"The slammer's no place for a Young Turk like you," she said. "You've got things to do."

"Yeah." He glanced up at her, still fire-engine red and blinking furiously against the threat of tears. After a moment his expression lightened a little and he managed a smile. "Yeah, I got things to do. And you too. I guess you like that Wheeler guy, huh?"

"Yes . . . I like him."

"So, you gonna stick around and date him or something?"

Or something, it seemed. "I don't know, Johnny. I just don't know. I've been thinking maybe I ought to go back to Berkeley—" At the boy's obvious distress she quickly added, "I haven't decided yet, of course."

His knitted brows said he truly didn't understand adults.

As they started toward her car Johnny glanced at her a couple of times. Cat thought he was still worried about her leaving and it nearly broke her heart. She wished she hadn't let her ambivalence slip.

And then suddenly a grin flashed on his face, full of adolescent intrigue and mischief. "Okay, what's the story?" he said. "Did you and Wheeler really get naked in the park?"

Cat was driving her Mustang down Main Street, her dark hair streaming in the sunlight, when a package of cheese puffs plopped into the passenger seat beside her. She checked out the pedestrians on the sidewalk, then craned around to look behind her, but saw no one she recognized.

The roar of an engine in the next lane brought her back around with a start. Gunning the motor of his Corvette, Blake pulled up precariously close to her. Smart alec, she thought, ignoring him. Some men couldn't take no for an answer.

She hit the gas and the Mustang jumped out in front.

But not for long.

He surged up, head to head with her instantly, burning up the pavement with his powerful machine. That car did everything but paw like a bull, she thought, flashing Blake a look that told him what she thought of his macho antics.

Unperturbed, he fenced with her for another block or two, then he hit the horn and waved her over. He wanted her to pull to the curb. She didn't budge from her lane.

He was unrelenting in his determination to force her over, but Cat wouldn't be intimidated. Mariner's Park was the next turn off, and perhaps for old times' sake, Cat decided to go for it. She pulled her car into the parking lot, screeched to a stop, leapt over the side of the convertible. And ran.

She was thankful she had on jeans and tennies. She was also thankful she could run like a thoroughbred. It was only when she got crazy and tried to leapfrog the birdbath that she sacrificed precious seconds. He tagged her as she darted through the picnic area, and they fell in the grass and rolled and rolled and rolled. She landed on her back, with him over her, breathing and laughing.

"Kinda like the three-legged race, huh?" he said.

"I let you catch me."

Cat fought to quiet the tumult inside her. He was devastating hovering above her. Just that, devastasting. She'd never seen him so gorgeous, his eyes hot and smoky, his body breathing sex. His tousled hair streamed with sunshine.

"*Let* me?" he said, laughing. "In that case I'll press my luck. How about an answer to my proposal?"

"Which proposal was that? The indecent one? Or the one in which marriage was mentioned?"

"Either," he said. "No, both."

"I cannot marry you, Blake. As for the other—"

"Wait—why not?" He pretended anger. "Why the

hell not? I got your client sprung, didn't I? Johnny's a free teenager."

"With my evidence," she reminded him.

"See what a team we make. By the way, Skip Sinclair will be cooling his heels for a while on robbery and assorted other charges. I gave his parents your card, counselor."

"Oh, thanks."

"Don't thank me, woman. Marry me."

"*Blake*, for starters, we have nothing in common." Undoubtedly she sounded as helpless as she felt. He'd been pursuing her mercilessly ever since she showed up on his doorstep with Bumper that night. Thrilling as it was, he had to be made to see that it couldn't work. For *his* sake.

He dug another package of puffs from his jacket and dangled them above her nose. "Nothing in common?"

She squirmed out from under him and sat up, determined to talk some sense into his stubborn head. "You have a career to think about, mister, a future."

"That's just it. I don't want to think about either without you."

She turned serious then. "I'd be a liability to you, Blake. We both know that."

"You'd be the best thing that ever happened to me, you knucklehead. I know some things about myself now that I didn't know before."

He pushed himself up and crouched in front of her, gripping her by the arms. "I really want to be the governor of this state, Cat. I think we could do it—even without a political machine to back us up. You know, the old grass roots approach. Winning an election because the *people* are behind you." His smile was irresistible. "I think that's a refreshing idea, don't you?"

"*We* could do it? Why we? Why *me*?"

He threw back his head and laughed.

Cat was astonished and a little frightened. She'd never seen him like this, ever. He was a wild man.

"Why you?" His eyes said she'd have to be crazy not to know. "Because I *love* you, woman. Madly! Because you're more than fire and fight, you're ballast. You'll keep me honest and remind me that I'm human. I *need* you, Catherine. What do you say to that?"

Help! That's what she said. Needed her? Loved her? *Madly?* Her heart was soaring, but she wasn't crazy enough to let him know it. "I'm not sure I like being called ballast."

Laughing, he gazed into her eyes. "I *do* need you, beautiful lady, but it's more than that. I've got a lot of making up to do for the last ten years. I want to turn your sadness into sunshine, I owe you that. I want to make you smile and hear your crazy, husky laughter every day of my life. Let me do that, will you, Cat? Let me make you happy."

He touched her face, an endearingly awkward caress, and his voice went husky. "The truth is I'd kind of like to be a hero again, in your eyes. And this time I want to deserve it."

"Oh . . . Blake—" She broke off, inexpressively touched. Tears misted her eyes and a tender barrier swelled in her throat. Seconds flew by, but she simply couldn't speak.

Blake watched her, mystified as she knuckled away tears and refused to look at him. Taking her silence as reluctance, he brought her head up. "You aren't going to force me to get physical, are you, Cat?" he said, only half-joking. He shook her gently, but with enough latent sexual desire to send the park up in flames.

"Okay—" She gasped more than said it.

"Yes?" His eyebrow cocked. "You will?"

Breathless, Cat pressed the heel of her hand to his chest like an outmatched prizefighter. His outpouring had almost totally overwhelmed her, but she desperately needed time to think this through! "I said *okay*—to the indecent proposal—*maybe* to that other thing." She swallowed thickly. "I'm not sure I want to be a politician's wife."

This time Blake took her reaction for exactly what it was. Resistance. She was a woman in want of more tangible persuasions. "Oh, I think you do," he said, laughing, flashing a silvery warning with his eyes. "In fact, I think you want it bad. I think you're dying to be a politician's wife."

Cat felt something seize up inside her as he caught hold of her hand and brought her fingers to his mouth. She felt the heat of his lips on her flesh, the sexy dart of his tongue.

His eyes said he could read her body's reaction, every sharp inner thrill she felt. "You want to be in my bed as much as I want you there, Cat. You want to make love, amazing love . . . and maybe some little politicians."

Little politicians?

"Say it, Cat. Say what I want to hear."

"I did . . . maybe."

"No, that other thing, that four-letter word."

A number of such words flashed through Cat's head, but she was pretty sure she knew the one he meant. Even the simple act of forming *that* word in her mind twisted her inside out with angst. It wasn't something she'd ever said before to a man. It wasn't something she'd ever felt for a man. But she was feeling it now—in the wild beat of her heart and the misty sting beneath her eyelids. She was coming apart inside, sweetly this time, irresistibly.

"Say it, Cat. I need to hear it from you."

She caught the soft flesh of her lower lip between her teeth. "I suppose I do lov—"

He pulled her into his arms before she could get the words out, nearly squeezing the breath out of her in his exuberance. "God, I love you!" he said, his voice shaking. "Do you know what you do to me? You open me up. You make me feel."

He pulled back to look at her and tenderness flared

in his eyes. Tenderness and such a sweet, hungry, sexy blast of love, she was rocked by it. Tears sparkled in her eyes and her lips trembled.

"I lov—" The words hiked up in Cat's throat again. He laughed, watching her, waiting.

"Oh, dammit, I l-love you," she blurted. "I *do* love you, I've *always* loved you"—her voice wobbled and cracked—"even when I hated you."

His low, rich laughter died on her lips. The kiss became a celebration as she flung her arms around his neck and abandoned herself to the joy flooding through her. She loved this man! It was crazy—the craziest thing that had ever happened to her, but she couldn't fight the feelings anymore.

Cat's sweet abandon was interrupted by the pointed sound of a throat clearing behind her. She broke the kiss, startled. A smile flickered in Blake's eyes as he glanced over her shoulder.

"It's the park police," he whispered.

Twisting around in Blake's arms, Cat met the frowning stare of the same policeman who'd interrupted their last rendezvous in the park. The officer nodded at her, then addressed himself to Blake.

"Excuse me, sir, but this *is* a public park."

Cat felt Blake's body jerk with laughter. She pinched him a good one, then turned her attention to the officer. "It's okay," she said, the soul of seriousness. "I'm going to marry him."

Coming next month . . .

Once Upon a Time . . . WHAT DREAMS MAY COME
by Kay Hooper

Kay Hooper has established herself as one of the few romance writers who can successfully blend elements of intrigue and mystery into her love stories . . . only to leave her legions of devoted fans clamoring for more. Here in the third of her *Once Upon a Time* stories, Kay weaves a spellbinding tale of a modern day Rip Van Winkle, a man who finds that in order to win the heart of his long lost childhood sweetheart, he must first help her track down the mysterious and dangerous man who has been pursuing her.

John Mitchell was in a coma for nine years following a tragic car accident one week before he was to marry Kelly Russell. He awakens to find his world irrevocably changed and Kelly nowhere to be found. After tracking her down for over a year he finally finds her and vows to win her back.

In the following excerpt John, nicknamed "Mitch," shows up at Kelly's house determined to prove that his love was forever.

Kelly was in the conservatory at the back of the house, gazing at white wicker furniture and lush green plants, when the doorbell sounded. Since she was expecting the delivery, via her new boss, of a computer system, she wasn't surprised by the sound.

She opened the heavy paneled oak door, expecting to see a delivery man with clipboard in hand and an inquiring look. And even though the newspaper article had at least prepared her for the possibility, she could feel the color drain from her face.

It was Mitch.

Taller than she remembered, his shoulders wider and heavier with maturity, a new look of strength and power in his stance. The gleaming dark sable hair had gone silver at the temples, but rather than making him look older, it, along with the black patch over his left eye, gave him an almost piratical air of danger.

"May I come in?" His voice was deeper than she remembered, slightly husky, and despite the prosiac request, she could hear the note of strain.

She stepped back wordlessly and opened the door wider, holding on so tightly to the ornate brass handle that she felt her nails biting into her palm. *Strangers,* she thought with the detachment that comes of total shock. *We're strangers.*

She pushed the door closed behind him as he came in, then led the way into the den, where a fire burned brightly in the stone fireplace. She didn't know what to say to him. Her legs felt shaky, and she sank down in a comfortable chair near the fire, watching as he slowly crossed the room and stood just a few feet away near the hearth.

"You knew I had come out of the coma." It wasn't a question.

Kelly answered anyway, her own voice holding tension. "I saw a newspaper article." She didn't mention that it had been only a week before.

"I'm sorry," she said suddenly, almost blurting it out. There was a flash in the dark, watching eye, as if some emotion had surged inside him, but his face remained expressionless.

"Sorry for what, Kelly? That you didn't wait for me? I've seen all the medical records; I know what they told you." But there was something in his voice that didn't jibe with the words, something that might have been bitterness.

She gestured helplessly, then let her hands fall back into her lap. "The weeks turned into months. Years." Her voice was toneless now. "The only thing I could think of doing was to keep going, the way we'd planned. Finish college, get a job. And wait. But they told me you'd never wake up. The doctors seemed so sure of that."

"When did you give up on me?" he asked, the question somehow very important.

Kelly didn't want to relive that period of her life, but she had to answer him. "It was after Dad died. You'd been in the coma nearly four years. Everyone else was gone. And it hurt so much to keep hoping."